A Journey through Time

A Journey through Time in Verse and Rhyme

Poems collected by Heather Thomas

Floris Books

First published in 1987
This revised edition published in 1998 by Floris Books

British Library CIP Data available

ISBN 0-86315-271-6

Printed in Great Britain by
The Bath Press, Bath

Contents

Foreword

It is important to be aware of the immense effect poetic language has on the growing child, whether through simple verse, rhyme and rhythm, or poetry at its most profound. Poetry should be spoken, for in the speaking the mood felt by the teacher will be passed to the children. Poetry, which must first enrich the feeling life, also fosters the ability to express and articulate clear and meaningful speech later on. This is so necessary for our chaotic times where words need to be strengthened through understanding. Words spoken from the heart with right will and right thought bring harmony into the world: this harmony works as a healing force in human nature.

This invaluable collection offers a wealth of verse for use by teachers at every stage of school life. The poems, which have been lovingly collected and used over the years by Heather Thomas, encompass moods of devotion and wonder, humour and joy, and provide support for the subject matter of lessons, acting as an aid to the growth and development of the children. Experience in the joy of sound extends beyond simply remembering words; it also helps to develop faculties which will hopefully awaken in children the desire to create for themselves. For the adult, too, this collection presents verses through which the meditative quality of the inner life can be stimulated, thereby enabling us to develop the true Word which lies at the heart of every human being.

Valerie Miles B.A.

Acknowledgments

Although every effort has been made to identify the authors of all the poems, this has not been possible in every case. Therefore, I would like to take this opportunity to offer my sincere apologies to anyone whose name I have not been able to put to their work. Omissions will be happily rectified in any future edition.

Welsh Incident by Robert Graves, from *Complete Poems,* by permission of Carcanet Press.

Norman and Saxon; Puck's Song; Eddi's Service by Rudyard Kipling by permission of A.P. Watt Ltd on behalf of The National Trust.

The Donkey by G.K. Chesterton by permission of A.P. Watt Ltd on behalf of The Royal Literary Fund.

Ducks' Ditty from *The Wind in the Willows* by Kenneth Grahame copyright The University Chest, Oxford, by permission of Curtis Brown, London.

I love all beauteous things reprinted from *Robert Bridges: Poetical Works* (1936) by permission of Oxford University Press.

The Snare; The Ancient Elf by James Stephens by permission of The Society of Authors for the estate of James Stephens.

Cargoes; A Creed by John Masefield by permission of The Society of Authors for the estate of John Masefield.

Loveliest of Trees by A.E. Housman by permission of The Society of Authors for the estate of A.E. Housman.

Five Eyes; Unstooping; Earth Folk; Trees; Some One; Silver; Eeka Neeka; Then; Martha; The Huntsmen; The Rainbow; Please to Remember; Tired Tim by permission of the Literary Trustees of Walter de la Mare, and the Society of Authors as their representative.

Far Over the Misty Mountains by J.R.R. Tolkien from *The Lord of the Rings,* by permission of HarperCollins Ltd.

Hallowe'en by Leonard Clark by permission of Robert Clark as literary executor.

The Llama; The Elephant by Hilaire Belloc by permission of the Peters Fraser & Dunlop Group Ltd.

I'm a Starling ... me Darling by Pam Ayres from *The Works,* BBC Books, © Pam Ayres 1992.

Night Mail by W.H.Auden by permission of Faber and Faber Ltd.

Light looked down and beheld darkness ... by Laurence Housman by permission of Jonathan Cape.

Stones, Rivers, Cliffs or Trees; Seasons; Snowflakes; Nocturne; Easter; Resurgence; With My Words; Alchemy; Lied from Heinrich von Ofterdingen by permission of David Kuhrt.

Night Sky; Word made Flesh by Kathleen Raine by permission of the author.

Introduction

The poems in this book have been published in response to requests from teachers who are beginning their work in Rudolf Steiner or Waldorf Education, and who are looking for poems and verses to enrich the experience of the main lesson and other subject lessons.

All teaching in these schools is based on the different needs of the children at each stage of their growth and inner development. In accordance with this I have tried to arrange the contents of the book in suitable order beginning with material for younger children, from the age of six plus. However, such an order cannot be strictly consistent as certain verses, for instance, for morning, evening or the seasons would be used at special times of the day or on special days throughout the year.

I have also included several verses for use by the teachers themselves which will help them in their understanding not only of children but of human nature in its manifold variety and diversity.

I hope that many parents, too, who have shared with their children the poems, puzzles, rhymes, riddles, word-games and so on, remembered from their own childhood, will be able to share once again in the joy experienced by their own children in meeting the old and new friends gathered here.

I would like to express my thanks to all those who have sent me poems and verses at one time or another, whether written by themselves or by someone else, and to all those authors who have granted permission for me to include their poems in this collection.

Also, to Jane Bishop of The Society of Authors for her help in tracing copyright; Magda Maier and Gundula Gombert for taking so much time and trouble to correct many of the poems and verses in both English and German; David Macgregor for his corrections; my colleagues at The Rudolf Steiner Waldorf School in Kings

Langley, Hertfordshire; and to the staff of Floris Books for preparing this revised edition for publication.

Last, but by no means least, I would like to express my deep gratitude to Dawn Golten because without her tireless efforts and endless patience it would not have been possible to bring this new edition to fruition. My most special thanks go to her for the painstaking and meticulous care with which she has carried through this task — a labour of love indeed.

Heather Thomas

This is the Key

This is the Key of the Kingdom;
In that Kingdom is a city;
In that city is a town;*
In that town there is a street;
In that street there winds a lane;
In that lane there is a yard;
In that yard there is a house;
In that house there waits a room;
In that room an empty bed;
And on that bed a basket —
A Basket of Sweet Flowers;
        Of Flowers, of Flowers;
        A Basket of Sweet Flowers.

Flowers in a Basket;
Basket on the bed;
Bed in the chamber;
Chamber in the house;
House in the weedy yard;
Yard in the winding lane;
Lane in the broad street;
Street in the high town;
Town in the city;
City in the Kingdom.
This is the key of the Kingdom.
        Of the Kingdom this is the Key.

* The heart of it, within the walls.

– – – ❖ – – –

Morning

– – – ❖ – – –

Morning Verse

ANONYMOUS

Oh what a joy is the morning sun
Shining with love now the night is gone —
See how it gleams, feel the earth grow warm,
Flowers are springing to greet the morn.
Birds they are singing in feathered flight,
Beasts they are moving with all their might,
And in my heart do I truly know
Nature and I by sun's grace must grow.

Tall as a tree I stand,
Far reach my roots in the earth,
Grows into bloom my love.

MOLLY DE HAVAS

Straight as a spear I stand,
Strength fills my legs and arms,
Warmth fills my heart with love.

"See!" said the bee,
"I can fly to the top of that very high tree!"
"Ah!" said the star, "I am above you high and far!"
"Ho!" said the gnome, "My home is in the stone!"

E E E, you see me.
A A A, here we are.
O O O, we do so.

Warm our hearts, O sun, and give
Light that we may daily live;
Growing as we ought to be,
True, and good, and strong, and free.

Good morning dear Earth
Good morning dear Sun
Good morning dear Trees and dear Flowers every one.
Good morning dear Beasts and Birds on the tree
Good morning to you and good morning to me.

JULIET COMPTON-BURNETT

I am myself; around me is the world,
Its flowers and leaves by golden sun unfurled.
All other people too say I and You
Firm earth beneath us and above the blue.

I Awaken Every Morning

TREVOR SMITH WESTGARTH

I awaken every morning
To the glory of the sun,
And the sunlight touches me
And the hearts of everyone,
And I lift up my heart
To the glory of the sun.

I awaken every morning
To the songbirds in the sky,
And I hear their lovely song
As along their way they fly,
And in my heart I rise
With the songbirds in the sky.

I awaken every morning
To the people that I know,
And I see in their eyes
All the love and care they show,
And I hold in my heart
All the people that I know.

EILEEN HUTCHINS

O Sun so bright
Thou giv'st thy light
And warming love
From heaven above
That life on earth
May come to birth.
May our eyes shine
With light like thine
May our hearts know
Thy warming glow;
May our hands give
Such strength to live
That we may be
A Sun, like thee.

The Golden Sun

ANONYMOUS

The golden sun so great and bright
Warms the world with all its might.
It makes the dark earth green and fair,
Attends each thing with ceaseless care.
It shines on blossom, stone and tree,
On bird and beast, on you and me.
Oh, may each deed throughout the day,
May everything we do and say
Be bright and strong and true,
Oh, golden sun, like you!

Verse

RUDOLF STEINER

I place myself steadfastly into existence
With certainty I tread the path of life
Love I nurse in the core of my being
Hope I lay into all my doing
Confidence I impress into my thinking.

Morning Prayer

RUDOLF STEINER

When I look at the sun, then I think God's spirit,
When I move my hand, then lives in me God's soul,
When I take a step, then stirs in me God's will.
And when I behold a man, then God's soul lives in him.
And so too it lives in father and mother,
In animal and flower, in tree and stone.
    Never can fear come near me
        If I think God's spirit;
        If I live God's soul;
        If I bestir God's will.

Night and Day

ANONYMOUS

In the night when stars are shining
And the moon sails through the sky,
When the children lay in slumber,
Soothed by gentle lullaby,
Angels with their golden pinions
Bear the sleeping souls on high.

In the morning at the sunrise
When the light of day does break,
Children's souls, by angels guided,
Sleep from rested body shake,
Ready now for work and learning,
Happy, steady and awake.

Morning

WILLIAM BLAKE

To find the Western path
Right thro the Gates of Wrath
I urge my way.
Sweet mercy leads me on
With soft repentant moan
I see the break of day.

The war of swords and spears
Melted by dewy tears
Exhales on high.
The sun is freed from fears
And with soft grateful tears
Ascends the sky.

The Song of the Earth's Dawn

From the Irish

Now comes the hour foretold, a God
 gift-bringing, a wonder-sight.
Is it a star new-born and splendid
 up-springing out of the night?
Is it a wave from the Fountain of Beauty
 up-flinging foam of delight?
Is it a glorious immortal bird that is
 winging hither its flight?
Is it a wave, high-crested, melodious,
 triumphant, breaking in light?
Is it a bloom, rose-hearted and joyous,
 a spendour risen from night?
Is it a flame from the world of the gods,
 and love runs before it,
 a quenchless delight?

Let the wave break,
Let the star rise,
Let the flame leap,

 Ours, if our hearts are wise,
 to take and keep.

Closing Verses for Main Lesson

ANONYMOUS

There lives in me an image
Of all that I should be;
Until I have become it
My heart is never free.

ANGELUS SILESIUS

Birds in the air;
Fishes in the water;
Stones on the land;
I'm in God's hand.

ANONYMOUS

I reverence the stars [*high Ah*]
I reverence the earth [*low Ah*]
I reverence man [*middle Ah*]
All the angels love me [*3 L's then E*]

[*Instructions on the right refer to eurythmy gestures that accompany the line*]

– – – ❖ – – –

Evening

– – – ❖ – – –

May Wisdom Shine

RUDOLF STEINER

May wisdom shine through me,
May love glow within me,
May strength permeate me,
That in me may arise
A helper of mankind
A server of holy things,
Selfless and true.

He who Illuminates

RUDOLF STEINER

He who illuminates the clouds
May He illuminate
May He penetrate
May He irradiate
And fill with light and warmth
Even us.

Evening Verse

RUDOLF STEINER

From my head to my feet
I am made in the image of God;
From my heart right into my hands
I feel the breath of God;
When I speak with my mouth
I follow the will of God.
When I behold God
In father and mother,
In all dear people,
In animal and plant,
In tree and stone,
Nothing can fill me with fear
But only with love
For all that is about me.

ALTERNATIVE TRANSLATION

From my head to my foot
I'm a picture of God,
From my heart to my hands
His own breath do I feel.
When I speak with my mouth
I shall follow God's will.
When I see and know God
In my father and mother,
In all dear, kind people,
In flowers and trees
And in birds, beast and stone,
Then no fear can come near.
Only love then will fill me
For all that is round me.

When at night I go to sleep
Six angels watch do keep,
Two my head are guarding,
Two my feet are guiding,
And two to whom is given
To guide my steps to heaven.

Verse

LAURENCE HOUSMAN

Light looked down and beheld darkness,
"Thither will I go," said Light.
Peace looked down and beheld war,
"Thither will I go," said Peace.
Love looked down and beheld hatred,
"Thither will I go," said Love.
    So came Light and shone,
    So came Peace and gave rest,
    So came Love and brought life,
And the Word was made flesh and dwelt among us.

From *The Rime of the Ancient Mariner*

SAMUEL TAYLOR COLERIDGE

He prayeth well, who loveth well,
Both man and bird and beast ...
He prayest best, who loveth best
All things both great and small;
For the dear God who loveth us,
He made and loveth all.

Night Sky

KATHLEEN RAINE

There came such clear opening of the night sky
The deep glass of wonders, the dark mind,
In unclouded gaze of the abyss
Opened like the expression of a face.
I looked into that clarity where all things are
End and beginning, and saw
My destiny there.

"So," I said, "no other
was possible ever. This
Is I. The pattern stands
so, for ever."

What am I? Bound and unbounded
A pattern among the stars, a point in motion
Tracing my way.

I am my way; it is I.
I travel among the wonders.
Held in that gaze and known
In the eye of the abyss.

"Let it be so," I said,
And my heart laughed with joy
To know the death I must die.

Nocturne

DAVID KUHRT

I heard the cold midnight mist whisper
On the water: Who is the moon,
Hanging yellowly there in the still night air?
The cold moon shimmered in the mist and sang
Silver memories of sunlight upon the water
Selflessly through the night.

Action Verses

Working

MOLLY DE HAVAS

The Farmer is sowing his seed,
    in the field he is sowing his seed.
The Reaper is cutting the hay,
    in the meadow is cutting the hay.
The Gardener is digging the ground,
    in the garden is digging the ground.
The Woodman is chopping the tree,
    in the forest is chopping the tree.
The Fisher is drawing his nets,
    in the sea he is drawing his nets.
The Builder is laying the bricks,
    in the wall he is laying the bricks.
The Cobbler is mending the shoes,
    in the shop he is mending the shoes.
The Miller is grinding the corn,
    in the mill he is grinding the corn.
The Baker is kneading the dough,
    in the kitchen he is kneading the dough.
The Mother is rocking her child,
    in her arms she is rocking her child.

The Dwarfs

ANONYMOUS

Pick and hammer each must hold,
Deep in earth to mine the gold;
Ready over each one's back,
Hangs a little empty sack.

When their hard day's work is done
Home again they march as one.
Full sacks make a heavy load
As they tramp along the road.

Little Dwarfs so short and strong
Heavy-footed march along;
Every head is straight and proud,
Every step is firm and loud.

The Cobbler

FRANCES B. WOOD

A merry cobbler man am I
You'll hear me sing as you pass by.

I cobble, cobble all day long,
And as I work I sing this song:

With tap, tap, tap, I heel and sole
With stitch, stitch, stitch, I make things whole.

No matter how much worn they be
Just send your boots and shoes to me.

Back they'll come as good as new;
Yes, I'm the cobbler man for you.

Song of the Fairy Shoemaker

From *The Leprechaun*

WILLIAM ALLINGHAM

Tick, tack, rip, rap
Ticka, tacka, too —
Scarlet leather sewn together
This will make a shoe.

Left, right, pull it tight
Summer days are warm
Underground in winter
Laughing at the storm.

Big boots for hunting
Sandals for the hall
White for a wedding
Pink for the ball.

This way, that way
So we make a shoe,
Getting quicker every minute
Ticka, tacka, too.

Blacksmith

B.K PYKE

All the night
And all day long
I hark to the sound
Of the blacksmith's song.

Red his fire —
The bright sparks fly
To dance with stars
In the joyous sky.

A Tragic Story

W.M. THACKERAY

There lived a sage in days of yore,
And he a handsome pigtail wore:
But wondered much and sorrowed more
    Because it hung behind him.

He mused upon this curious case,
And swore he'd change the pigtail's place,
And have it hanging at his face,
    Not dangling there behind him.

Says he, "The mystery I've found —
I'll turn me round" — he turned him round;
    But still it hung behind him.

And right and left, and round about,
And up and down, and in and out,
He turned; but still the pigtail stout
    Hung steadily behind him.

And though his efforts never slack,
And though he twist, and twirl, and tack,
Alas! still faithful to his back,
    The pigtail hangs behind him.

Then round, and round, and out and in,
All day the puzzled sage did spin;
In vain — it mattered not a pin —
    The pigtail hung behind him.

Footsteps

ANONYMOUS

The foxes move so softly that we do not hear a sound.
The trotting horses' hoof-beats ring out loudly on the ground.
And litttle lambs in springtime gaily skip around and round.

Spiral

Let us make a little visit to the curly house of Snail.
Round we go until we find him hidden in his coat of mail,
Then we turn and go back homeward still a-winding all the way,
Till we come out from his tunnel to the sunny light of day.

The Snail

Slowly, slowly, like a snail, I move towards the corner.
Silent, silent, very quiet, going to the corner.
Creeping, creeping, on my way, at last I reach the corner.

The Huntsmen

WALTER DE LA MARE

Three jolly gentlemen,
    In coats of red,
Rode their horses
    Up to bed.

Three jolly gentlemen
    Snored till morn,
Their horses champing
    The golden corn.

Three jolly gentlemen,
    At break of day,
Came clitter-clatter down the stairs
    And galloped away.

The Knight

MOLLY DE HAVAS

I ride on my horse with my sword in my hand,
I ride through the wooded and mountainous land.
I battle with dragons, with giants I fight;
Defending the weak and upholding the right.

My sword is of steel and my helmet of gold,
I dare all adventures, my heart is so bold.
My armour is shining as bright as the light,
And I am a gallant and glorious Knight.

Sir Nicketty Nox

HUGH CHESTERMAN

Sir Nicketty Nox was an ancient knight,
So old was he that he'd lost his sight.
Blind as a mole, and slim as a fox,
And dry as a stick was Sir Nicketty Nox.

His sword and buckler were old and cracked,
So was his charger and that's a fact.
Thin as a rake from head to hocks,
Was this rickety nag of Sir Nicketty Nox.

A wife he had and daughters three,
And all were as old, as old could be.
They mended the shirts and darned the socks
Of that old Antiquity, Nicketty Nox.

Sir Nicketty Nox would fly in a rage
If anyone tried to guess his age.
He'd mouth and mutter and tear his locks,
This very pernickety Nicketty Nox.

The Stork

ANONYMOUS

I lift my leg, I stretch my leg,
    I plant it firm and light.
I lift again, and stretch again,
    My pace exactly right.
With care I go, so grand and slow,
    I move just like a stork;
My eye is bright, my head upright,
    And pride is in my walk.

The Journey

All round the great world we will go in our journey,
On lands and wide oceans we seek our adventures,
Then back to our own little circle of homeland.

Arms

ANONYMOUS

I lift my arms to the clear blue sky
I stretch them wide and I stretch them high.
Firmly on the earth I stand
To my neighbour I give my hand:
A friend to the left and a friend to the right,
God will keep me in his sight.

Clapping

Clap up, clap down, clap behind and clap before;
Clap up, clap down as we've often done before.

[*Starting slowly, getting faster, then slow to end*]

The Rider

ANONYMOUS

Little right and little left foot
Hark to what I have to say!
You shall leap like prancing horses
Gallop, gallop, far away!
Then we march like little soldiers,
Or like Puss on velvet paws.
Do not shuffle, do not scuffle!
Now I pray you be quite still!
For this is the rider's will.
Who then is the rider — tell! (I am)
Ah! you know his name quite well.

Brave and true will I be
Each good deed sets me free
Each kind word makes me strong;
I will fight for the right
I will conquer the wrong.

CHRISTINA ROSSETTI

Mix a pancake, stir a pancake,
Pop it in the pan:
Fry the pancake, toss the pancake,
Catch it if you can.

If a task is once begun
Never leave it 'till it's done;
Be the labour great or small,
Do it well or not at all.

The Old Woman and the Apples

The apples were ripe and ready to drop,
    UM — AH — ready to drop.
There came an old woman to pick 'em all up,
    UM — AH — pick 'em all up.
Down came a great apple and gave her a knock,
Which made the old woman go hippity hop.

If

P.A. ROPES

If I were oh, so very tall,
    I'd walk among the trees,
And bend to pick the topmost leaf
    As easy as you please.

If I were oh, so very small,
    I'd hide myself away,
And creep into a peony cup
    To spend the summer's day.

Anapest

ANONYMOUS

I am strong, I am brave, I am valiant and bold,
For the sun fills my heart with his life-giving gold.
I am helpful and truthful and loving and free,
For my heart's inner sunshine glows brightly in me.
I will open my heart to the sunbeams so bright;
I will warm all the world with my heart's inner light.

Will

MOLLY DE HAVAS

I can turn myself and turn myself
Or curl up when I will,
I can stand on tiptoe reaching high
Or hold myself quite still.

ANONYMOUS

The little furry rabbits
Keep very, very still,
They peep at me across the grass
As I go up the hill.
But if I venture nearer
To watch them at their play,
A flash of white and they are gone
Not one of them will stay.

The Queen of Hearts

TRADITIONAL

The queen of hearts she made some tarts
All on a summer's day;
The knave of hearts he stole those tarts
And took them right away.
The king of hearts called for the tarts
And beat the knave full sore.
The knave of hearts brought back the tarts
And vowed he'd steal no more.

Stepping Rhythms

Grandad walks slow: 1 2 3 4
Father marches onward so: 1 2 3 4 5 6 7 8
Little children pitter patter, clitter clatter, chitter chatter.
Grandad walks slow: etc.

[*For changing speeds*]

I laugh, ha ha, I laugh he he,
I laugh all day, it pleases me.

Jack be nimble, Jack be quick,
Jack jump over the candle stick.

Walking the Alphabet

TREVOR SMITH WESTGARTH

A B C D E F G
Sing the alphabet with me

H I J K L M N
We'll sing it again and again

O P Q R S T U
Fun for me and fun for you

U V W X Y Z
Now the alphabet's been said.

[*To the tune of* Twinkle, Twinkle little star:
Repeat first four bars of tune for H I J K L M N]

Painting Verse

ROBERT LEWERS

Help me dear Angels of the light
With tender care to paint aright
The colours that in me arise
Bringing to earth from out the skies.
Help me to see in Earth's dark ways
The golden sword of Michael raised;
From out my heart I, too, would bring
The colours of the rainbow ring.

❖

Finger Games

❖

A Little Finger Game

E.J. FALCONER

Here is a house with a pointed door
[*Index fingers and thumbs together for pointed door*]
Windows tall, and a fine flat floor.
[*Fingers of both hands joined at the tips and stretched apart for windows, hands held flat, palms down, side by side for floor*]
Three good people live in the house.
[*Three middle fingers of one hand standing up under shelter of the other*]
One fat cat, and one thin mouse.
[*Right-hand thumb stands up for cat, right-hand little finger stands up for mouse*]
Out of his hole the mousie peeps
[*Right-hand little finger peeps through left-hand folded into a fist*]
Out of his corner the pussy-cat leaps!
[*Right-hand thumb jumps over left-hand fist*]
Three good people say "Oh, oh, oh!"
Three fingers stand up as before]
Mousie inside says "No, no, no!"
[*Little finger draws back inside left-hand fist*]

Two and two go out together
Three and three
And one and one.
Very very clever little pinky,
But cleverest of all is the big fat thumb.

[*Sideways movement of fingers, in groups, both hands together. Last line: thumb dances then goes down, then up!*]

Ten little squirrels sat on a tree.
[*Show ten fingers*]
The first two said, "Why what do we see?"
[*Hold up thumbs*]
The next two said, "A man with a gun."
[*Forefingers*]
The next two said, "Let's run, let's run."
[*Middle fingers*]
The next two said, "Let's hide in the shade."
[*Ring fingers*]
The next two said, "Why? We're not afraid."
[*Little fingers*]
Then "BANG" went the gun and away they all ran.
[*Clap loudly and hide all fingers behind back*]

Dance, Thumbkin, dance.
Dance, Thumbkin, dance.
Dance my merry men every one
But Thumbkin he can dance alone
So dance, Thumbkin, dance.

[*Then the same with Foreman, Longman, Ringman, Littleman*]

TRADITIONAL

Here's the church and here's the steeple
Look inside and see all the people.
Here's the minister going upstairs,
And here's the minister saying his prayers.

TREVOR SMITH WESTGARTH

Babies walk upstairs
One step at a time
Boys and girls race up and down
As fast as lightning climb.
Old men often slip and slide
On their way to bed,
Ladies step so quietly
You can hardly hear their tread.

TREVOR SMITH WESTGARTH

Here is a castle
With four tall towers.
Here's a little cottage
With a garden full of flowers.
Here is a sentry box
A soldier stands inside,
And here is a tiny hole
Where a mouse can sleep and hide.

– – – ❖ – – –

Skipping

– – – ❖ – – –

Traditional Skipping Rhymes

Teddybear, teddybear, turn around,
Teddybear, teddybear, touch the ground.
Teddybear, teddybear, go upstairs,
Teddybear, teddybear, say your prayers.
Teddybear, teddybear, switch off the light,
Teddybear, teddybear, say "Good night."

GERMAN VERSION:

Teddiebär, Teddiebär, dreh dich um,
Teddiebär, Teddiebär, mach dich krumm.
Teddiebär, Teddiebär, zeig dein' Fuss,
Teddiebär, Teddiebär, mach ein' Gruss.
Teddiebär, Teddiebär, Augen zu,
Teddiebär, Teddiebär, wie alt bist du?
Eins, zwei drei, usw.

All the girls in our town lead a happy life
Except for ... who wants to be a wife.
A wife she may be — according to me
Along comes ... as happy as can be.
She hugs him, she kisses him, she sits upon his knee
And says "O my darling, won't you marry me."
Yes, no, ... etc.

Winter and Spring

TREVOR SMITH WESTGARTH

Winter gently lays its blanket soft of snow [*stamp*]
While slowly underneath the bulbs all start to grow. [*stamp*]

Spring comes springing, laughing, singing, [*skip*]
Waking, warming, daffodiling. [*skip*]

Winter slowly says goodbye [*stamp*]
While icicles begin to cry. [*stamp*]

Primrose, violet — all are growing [*skip*]
Shoots above the earth are showing. [*skip*]

Winter's chill now cannot freeze [*stamp*]
Catkins hang upon the trees. [*skip*]

Winter dies [*stamp*]
Spring's alive. [*skip*]

Winter dies [*stamp*]
Spring's alive. [*skip*]

Winter dies [*stamp*]
Spring's alive. [*skip*]

❖

Fables

❖

The Fox and the Grapes

A FABLE BY AESOP

"What luscious grapes," said a hungry fox;
"What fine, good grapes," said he.
"If I jump as high as a clever fox can
I'll have those grapes for tea."

So he jumped and he leaped and he snapped with his teeth,
But only the air could he bite,
While the grapes, sweet and juicy, dangled above,
And swayed at a lofty height.

The fox grew mad, and scarlet red,
But tossing his head, said he:
"Those grapes are sour and full of worms —
Who wants those grapes? Not me!"

The Donkey

A FABLE BY AESOP

The donkey had a basket full,
A basket full of salt,
Across the stream did master pull,
But donkey made a fault.

He fell into the water deep,
And all the salt was lost;
This trick the donkey did repeat
But to the master's cost.

The basket now was filled again
With sponges to the brim,
And when he tried his trick again
The donkey found it grim.

The Shepherd Boy and the Wolf

A FABLE BY AESOP

A shepherd boy beside a stream,
"The wolf, the wolf," was wont to scream;
And when the villagers appeared
He'd laugh and call them silly-eared.

A wolf at last came down the steep:
"The wolf, the wolf, my legs, my sheep!"
The creature had a jolly feast,
Quite undisturbed, on boy and beast.
For none believes the liar forsooth,
Even when the liar speaks the truth.

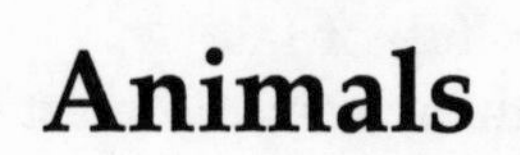

Animals

- - - ❖ - - -

A Cloak for a Fairy

ANONYMOUS

Spider, Spider, what are you spinning?
A cloak for a fairy, I'm just beginning.
What is it made of, tell me true?
Threads of moonshine, pearls of dew!
When will the fairy be wearing it?
Tonight, when the glow worms' lamps are lit.
Can I see her if I come peeping?
All good children must then be sleeping.

The Spider

CHRISTINA T. OWEN

I watched a little spider build a silvery house so fine;
He spun with his own silken thread a beautiful design.
Up he went and down he went, round and round and round;
Across he went, and back he went, making not a sound.
In he went and out he went, weaving to and fro,
Spinning fast until he had a fine new house to show.

Robin Redbreast

TRADITIONAL

Little Robin Redbreast
Sat upon a tree,
He sang merrily,
As merrily as could be.
He nodded with his head,
And his tail waggled he,
As little Robin Redbreast
Sat upon a tree.

Welcome, little Robin,
With your scarlet breast,
In this winter weather
Cold must be your nest.
Hopping on the carpet,
Picking up the crumbs,
Robin knows the children
Love him when he comes.

The Robin

LAURENCE ALMA TADEMA

When father takes his spade to dig
    Then Robin comes along;
He sits upon a little twig
    And sings a little song.

Or, if the trees are rather far,
    He does not stay alone,
But comes up close to where we are
    And bobs upon a stone.

Cock Robin

TRADITIONAL

Who killed Cock Robin?
"I," said the sparrow,
"With my bow and arrow,
I killed Cock Robin."

Who saw him die?
"I," said the fly,
"With my little eye,
I saw him die."

Who'll toll the bell?
"I," said the bull,
"Because I can pull,
I'll toll the bell."

Who'll dig his grave?
"I," said the owl,
"With my little trowel,
I'll dig his grave."

Who'll be the parson?
"I," said the rook,
"With my bell and book,
I'll be the parson."

Who'll be chief mourner?
"I," said the dove,
"I mourn for my love,
I'll be chief mourner."

Little Bird

Once a little bird went hop, hop, hop,
And I said, "little bird, will you stop, stop, stop."
I ran to the window to say "how do you do?"
But she shook her little tail and away she flew.

The Robin's Song

OLD ENGLISH RHYME

God bless the field and bless the furrow,
Stream and branch and rabbit burrow;
Hill and stone and flower and tree,
From Bristol town to Wetherby —
Bless the sun and bless the sleet,
Bless the lane and bless the street,
Bless the night and bless the day
From Somerset and all the way
To the meadows of Cathay;
Bless the minnow, bless the whale,
Bless the rainbow and the hail,
Bless the nest and bless the leaf,
Bless the righteous and the thief,
Bless the wing and bless the fin,
Bless the air I travel in,
Bless the mill and bless the mouse,
Bless the miller's bricken house,
Bless the earth and bless the sea,
God bless you and God bless me!

A Little Bird

CHRISTINA T. OWEN

A little bird perched on a limb;
He looked at me — I looked at him.
He flipped his tail and cocked his head;
"I've flown a long, long way," he said.

Last fall before the winter storms
I flew far south where it was warm.
Now I've come back again to sing
This happy news to you: "It's spring!"

Mice

ROSE FYLEMAN

I think mice
are rather nice.
Their tails are long,
their faces small,
They haven't any
chins at all.
Their ears are pink,
their teeth are white,
They run about
the house at night.
They nibble things
they shouldn't touch
And no one seems
to like them much.
But I think mice
are nice.

Six Little Mice

Six little mice sat down to spin,
Pussy passed by, and she peeped in.
"What are you at, my little men?"
"Making coats for gentlemen."
"Shall I come in and bite off your threads?"
"Oh, no, Miss Pussy, you'll snip off our heads."
"Oh, no, I'll not, I'll help you to spin."
"That may be so, but you don't come in!"

The Kind Mousie

NATALIE JOAN

There once was a cobbler
And he was so wee
That he lived in a hole
In a very big tree.
He had a good neighbour,
And she was a mouse —
She did his wee washing
And tidied his house.

Each morning at seven
He heard a wee tap,
And in came the mouse
In her apron and cap.
She lighted his fire
And she fetched a wee broom,
And she swept and she polished
His little Tree-room.

To take any wages
She'd always refuse,
So the cobbler said "Thank you!"
And mended her shoes;
And the owl didn't eat her,
And even the cat
Said "I never would catch
A kind mousie like that!"

Three Mice

CHARLOTTE DRUITT COLE

Three little mice walked into town,
Their coats were grey, and their eyes were brown.
Three little mice went down the street,
With woolwork slippers upon their feet.
Three little mice sat down to dine
On curranty bread and gooseberry wine.
Three little mice ate on and on,
Till every crumb of the bread was gone.
Three little mice, when the feast was done,
Crept home quietly one by one.
Three little mice went straight to bed,
And dreamt of crumbly, curranty — bread.

Cheetie-Poussie-Cattie, O

TRADITIONAL

There was a wee bit mousikee,
That lived in Gilberaty, O;
It couldna get a bit o cheese,
For Cheetie — Poussie — Catti, O.

I said unto the cheesikie,
"O fain wad I be at ye, O,
If it werena for the cruel paws
O Cheetie — Poussie — Cattie, O."

Five Eyes

WALTER DE LA MARE

In Hans' old Mill his three black cats
Watch his bins for thieving rats.
Whisker and claw, they crouch in the night,
Their five eyes smouldering green and bright:
Squeaks from the flour sacks, squeaks from where

The cold wind stirs on the empty stair,
Squeaking and scampering, everywhere.
Then down they pounce, now in, now out,
At whisking tail, and sniffing snout;
While lean old Hans he snores away
Till peep of light at break of day;
Then up he climbs to his creaking mill,
Out come his cats all grey with meal —
Jekkel, and Jessup, and one-eyed Jill.

A Kitten's World

LEA WILLS *(aged 11)*

When she sleeps she looks dead as night;
When she's awake she's dynamite —
Her nose is as pink as a rose
She wears fur and no clothes.

Her tongue is as rough as a bristled brush
And she is always in a rush.
She runs off to have a play
And gets ready to pounce on her prey.

When she is proud she holds her head.
Sometimes at night she never goes to bed.
When she's hot she lays down a lot
On her back she has a white spot.

When she is angry she growls,
When she is lonely she howls.
When breakfast is nearly hers
She paces about and purrs.

As her little eyes drop closed
And the pinkness goes out of her nose
She goes to the land of dreams;
When she sees us again her face beams.

Lion and Unicorn

TRADITIONAL

The lion and the unicorn
Were fighting for the crown;
The lion beat the unicorn
All round the town.

Some gave them white bread
And some gave them brown;
Some gave them plum cake,
And sent them out of town.

The Lion

ANONYMOUS

King of Beasts, the Lion,
Has velvet-padded paws.
Majestic mane to crown his head
And strong and cavernous jaws.

The lioness is hunter,
The cubs in shelter hide.
The mighty male remains
To be protector of the pride.

The Tyger

WILLIAM BLAKE

Tyger Tyger, burning bright
In the forests of the night,
What immortal hand or eye
Could frame thy fearful symmetry?

In what distant deeps or skies
Burnt the fire of thine eyes?
On what wings dare he aspire?
What the hand, dare seize the fire?

And what shoulder, and what art,
Could twist the sinews of thy heart?
And when thy heart began to beat,
What dread hand? and what dread feet?

What the hammer? what the chain?
In what furnace was thy brain?
What the anvil? what dread grasp
Dare its deadly terrors clasp?

When the stars threw down their spears
And water'd heaven with their tears,
Did he smile his work to see?
Did he who made the Lamb make thee?

Tyger Tyger, burning bright
In the forests of the night,
What immortal hand or eye
Dare frame thy fearful symmetry?

The Waddlers

OLIN WANNAMAKER

Said the Drake to his Lady
One very wet day
While he and she waddled
And splashed on their way:

"You really should know
How absurd you appear!
If you could just see
Yourself from the rear!

You rock and you roll
From left side to right,
You slap your feet down —
Oh, you are a sight!"

The Drake walked ahead
And duck fell behind,
And watching him closely,
She said: "He is blind!

The way that he waddles
He charges to me!
My dignified walk
He simply can't see.

But, rocking and rolling
In side to side sway,
He actually dreams
That I walk that way!"

She paused for a moment
To shake her tail dry,
Then paddled along
With a very deep sigh.

"No chance to correct him,"
She said: "I won't try!"

Duck's Ditty

KENNETH GRAHAME

All along the backwater,
    Through the rushes tall,
Ducks are a-dabbling,
    Up tails all!

Ducks' tails, drakes' tails
    Yellow feet a-quiver,
Yellow bills all out of sight
    Busy in the river!

Slushy green undergrowth
    Where the roach swim —
Here we keep our larder
    Cool and full and dim!

Everyone for what he likes!
    WE like to be
Heads down, tails up,
    Dabbling free!

High in the blue above
    Swifts whirl and call —
WE are down a-dabbling,
    Up tails all!

The Browy Hen

IRENE F. FAWSEY

A browny hen sat on her nest
    With a hey-ho for the springtime!
Seven brown eggs 'neath her downy breast
    With a hey-ho for the springtime!

A brown hen clucks all day from dawn,
    With a hey-ho for the springtime!
She's seven wee chicks as yellow as corn,
    With a hey-ho for the springtime!

Peacocks

ANONYMOUS

Peacocks sweep the fairies' rooms,
They use their folded tails for brooms.
But fairy dust is brighter far
Than any mortal colours are.
And all about their tails it clings
In strange designs of rounds and rings
And that is why they strut about
And proudly spread their feathers out.

The Eagle

ALFRED, LORD TENNYSON

He clasps the crag with crooked hands;
Close to the sun in lonely lands,
Ringed with the azure world, he stands.

The wrinkled sea beneath him crawls;
He watches from his mountain walls,
And like a thunderbolt he falls.

Mighty Eagle

PERCY BYSSHE SHELLEY

Mighty eagle! thou that soarest
O'er the misty mountain forest,
    And amid the light of morning
Like a cloud of glory highest,
And when night descends defiest
    The embattled tempests' warning!

From *The Skylark*

JAMES HOGG

Bird of the wilderness,
Blithesome and cumberless
Sweet by thy matin o'er moorland and lea!
Emblem of happiness,
Blest is thy dwelling-place —
O to abide in the desert with thee!

O'er fell and fountain sheen,
O'er moor and mountan green,
O'er the red streamer that heralds the day,
Over the cloudlet dim,
Over the rainbow's rim,
Musical cherub, soar, singing away!

Song of the Sylphs

EILEEN HUTCHINS

As we fly, as we fly,
On the wings of the light,
With the clouds through the sky,
With the wind in its flight:
All the birds in their winging
Will follow our way,
As they greet with their singing
The light and the day.

I'm a Starling ... me Darling

PAM AYRES

We're starlings, the missis, meself and the boys
We don't go round hoppin', we walks,
We don't go in for this singing all day
And twittering about, we just squawks.

We don't go in for these fashionable clothes
Like old Missel Thrush, and his spots,
Me breast isn't red, there's no crest on me head,
We've got sort of, hardwearing ... dots.

We starlings, the missis, meself and the boys,
We'll eat anything that's about,
Well anything but that old half coconut,
I can't hold it still. It falls out.

What we'd rather do, is wait here for you,
To put out some bread for the tits,
And then when we're certain, you're there by the curtain,
We flocks down and tears it to bits.

But we starlings, the missis, meself and the boys,
We reckon that we're being got at,
You think for two minutes, them finches and linnets,
You never see them being shot at.

So the next time you comes out, to sprinkle the crumbs out,
And there's starlings there, making a noise,
Don't you be so quick, to heave half a brick,
It's the missus, meself and the boys!

Whisky Frisky

TRADITIONAL

Whisky Frisky,
Hipperty hop,
Up he goes
To the tree top.

Whirly twirly
Round and round
Down he scampers
To the ground.

Furly, curly
What a tail,
Tall as a feather,
Broad as a snail.

Where's his supper?
In the shell.
Snappy, cracky,
Out it fell.

The Hedgehog

EDITH KING

The hedgehog is a little beast
Who likes a quiet wood,
Where he can feed his family
On proper hedgehog food.

He has a funny little snout
That's rather like a pig's,
With which he smells, like us, of course,
But also runts and digs.

He wears the queerest prickle coat,
Instead of hair or fur,
And only has to curl himself
To bristle like a burr.

He does not need to battle with
Or run away from foes,
His coat does all the work for him,
It pricks them on the nose.

The Beaver's Tale

From *The Green Frog and Other Stories*

ERLE WILSON

Our fathers when lodges they made
Had only their teeth and their claws,
When building their dams in the glade
They laboured alone in the shade,
For they had no community laws;
For they had no community laws.

But beavers today have an easier way
When building a village of wattle and clay
Each works for his neighbour —
It lightens the labour
And makes for the general good.
I'm sure if you'd try it
You'd never deny it's
The best of all laws for the wood.

The Little Hare

ANONYMOUS

Between the valley and the hill
There sat a little hare
He nibbled at the grass — until
The ground was nearly bare.

And when the ground was nearly bare
He rested in the sun.
A hunter came and saw him there
And shot him with his gun.

He thought he must be dead — be dead,
But wonderful to say
He found he was alive instead
And quickly ran away.

Our Night Visitor

Christina T. Owen

A bunny came to call last night.
I did not see him — that is right.
But he was there; here's how I know —
He nibbled at my carrot row.

The Snare

James Stephens

I hear a sudden cry of pain!
There is a rabbit in a snare;
Now I hear the cry again,
But I cannot tell from where.

But I cannot tell from where
He is calling out for aid!
Crying on the frightened air,
Making everything afraid!

Making everything afraid!
Wrinkling up his little face!
And he cries again for aid;
And I cannot find the place!

And I cannot find the place
Where his paw is in the snare!
Little one! Oh, little one!
I am searching everywhere!

The Shepherd

WILLIAM BLAKE

How sweet is the Shepherd's sweet lot!
From the morn to the evening he strays;
He shall follow his sheep all the day,
And his tongue shall be filled with praise.

For he hears the lamb's innocent call,
And he hears the ewe's tender reply;
He is watchful while they are in peace,
For they know when their Shepherd is nigh.

The Pig's Tail

NORMAN AULT

A furry coat has the bear to wear,
    The tortoise a coat of mail,
The yak has more than his share of hair,
    But — the pig has the curly tail.

The elephant's tusks are sold for gold,
    The slug leaves a silver trail,
The parrot is never too old to scold,
    But — the pig has the curly tail.

The lion can either roar or snore,
    The cow gives milk in a pail,
The dog can guard a door, and more,
    But — the pig has the curly tail.

The monkey makes you smile a while,
    The tiger makes you quail,
The fox has many a wile of guile,
    But — the pig has the curly tail.

For the rest of the beasts that prey or play,
    From tiny mouse to the whale,
There's much that I could say today,
    But — the pig has the curly tail.

The Donkey

G.K. Chesterton

When fishes flew and forests walk'd
And figs grew upon the thorn,
Some moment when the moon was blood
Then surely I was born;

With monstrous head and sickening cry
And ears like errant wings,
The devil's walking parody
On all four-footed things.

The tatter'd outlaw of the earth,
Of ancient crooked will;
Starve, scourge, deride me: I am dumb,
I keep my secret still.

Fools! For I also had my hour;
One far fierce hour and sweet:
There was a shout about my ears,
And palms before my feet.

The Llama

Hilaire Belloc

The llama is a woolly sort of fleecy hairy goat,
With an indolent expression and an undulating throat
Like an unsuccessful literary man.
And I know the place he lives in (or at least — I think I do)
It is Ecuador, Brazil or Chile — possibly Peru;
You must find it in the Atlas if you can.
The Llama of the Pampasses you never should confound
(In spite of a deceptive similarity of sound)
With the Lhama who is Lord of Turkestan,
For the former is a beautiful and valuable beast,
But the latter is not lovable nor useful in the least;
And the Ruminant is preferable surely to the Priest
Who battens on the woeful superstitions of the East,
The Mongol of the Monastery of Shan.

Ox and Cow

MARGARET MORGAN

Ox and Cow,
Behold them now;
Behold what work they do.

The cow, placid and gentle,
She chews the whole day through.
All day long she chews the cud,
Working miracles for mankind's good.

Ox and Cow,
Behold them now;
Behold what work they do.

The ox is a beast of burden,
He toils the whole day through.
Pulling the plough as best he can;
Bearing heavy loads for man.

Ox and Cow behold them now,
Behold what work they do;
Each give their gifts to help mankind;
Such selfless work they do.

Cows

JAMES REEVES

Half the time they munched the grass and all the time they lay
Down in the water-meadows, the lazy month of May.
A-chewing,
A-mooing,
To pass the hours away.
"Nice weather," said the brown cow.
"Ah," said the white.
"Grass is very tasty."
"Grass is all right."

Half the time they munched the grass and all the time they lay
Down in the water-meadows, the lazy month of May.
A-chewing,
A-mooing,
To pass the hours away.

"Rain coming," said the brown cow.
"Ah," said the white.
"Flies is very tiresome."
"Flies bite!"

Cows

PELHAM S. MOFFAT

Now the gentle cows are standing
Knee-deep in the dewy grass.
Dawn has found them, patient shadows,
Watching hours that softly pass.

Moving slowly over meadows,
Munching quiet unhurried ways,
They have nought to do but wander
Down the rich unheeded days.

Yet they bring about a wonder
Such as not the wisest can,
Changing common meadow grasses
Into richest food of man.

As they lie unmindful, chewing,
By a faintly sounding stream,
What new marvels are they viewing?
What deep secrets do they dream?

The Blind Men and the Elephant

JOHN GODFREY SAXE

It was six men of Hindostan,
To learning much inclined,
Who went to see the elephant,
(Though all of them were blind):
That each by observation
Might satisfy his mind.

The *first* approached the Elephant
    And happening to fall
Against his broad and sturdy side,
    At once began to bawl:
"Bless me, it seems the Elephant
    Is very like a wall."

The *second* feeling of his tusk,
    Cried, "Ho! what have we here
So very round and smooth and sharp?
    To me tis mighty clear
This wonder of an elephant
    Is very like a spear."

The *third* approached the animal
    And happening to take
The squirming trunk within his hands,
    Then boldly up and spake:
"I see," quoth he, "the Elephant
    Is very like a snake."

The *fourth* stretched out his eager hand
    And felt about the knee,
"What most this mighty beast is like
    Is mighty plain," quoth he;
"Tis clear enough the Elephant
    Is very like a tree."

The *fifth* who chanced to touch the ear
    Said, "Even the blindest man
Can tell what this resembles most;
    Deny the fact who can,
This marvel of an Elephant
    Is very like a fan."

The *sixth* no sooner had begun
    About the beast to grope,
Than, seizing on the swinging tail
    That fell within his scope,
"I see," cried he, "the Elephant
    Is very like a rope."

And so these men of Hindostan
    Disputed loud and long,
Each in his own opinion
    Exceeding stiff and strong,
Though *each* was *partly* in the right
    AND ALL WERE IN THE WRONG.

The Elephant

HILAIRE BELLOC

When people call this beast to mind,
They marvel more and more
At such a *little* tail behind
So *large* a trunk before.

The Lobster Quadrille

LEWIS CARROLL

"Will you walk a little faster?" said a whiting to a snail,
"There's a porpoise close behind us, and he's treading on my tail.
See how eagerly the lobsters and the turtles all advance!
They are waiting on the shingle — will you come and join the dance?
Will you, won't you, will you, won't you, will you join the dance?
Will you, won't you, will you, won't you, won't you join the dance?"

"You can really have no notion how delightful it will be
When they take us up and throw us, with the lobsters, out to sea!"
But the snail replied, "Too far, too far!" and gave a look askance —
Said he thanked the whiting kindly, but he would not join the dance.
Would not, could not, would not, could not, would not join the dance,
Would not, could not, would not, could not, could not join the dance.

"What matters it how far we go?" his scaly friend replied.
"There is another shore, you know, upon the other side.
The further off from England the nearer is to France —
Then turn not pale, beloved snail, but come and join the dance.
Will you, won't you, will you, won't you, will you join the dance?
Will you, won't you, will you, won't you, won't you join the dance?"

How doth the little Crocodile

LEWIS CARROLL

How doth the little crocodile
    Improve his shining tail,
And pour the waters of the Nile
    On every golden scale!

How cheerfully he seems to grin,
    How neatly spreads his claws,
And welcomes little fishes in,
    With gently smiling jaws!

The Owl and the Pussy Cat

EDWARD LEAR

The Owl and the Pussy Cat went to sea
In a beautiful pea-green boat,
They took some honey, and plenty of money,
Wrapped up in a five-pound note.
The Owl looked up to the stars above,
And sang to a small guitar:
"O lovely Pussy! O Pussy my love,
What a beautiful Pussy you are,
You are, You are!
What a beautiful Pussy you are!"

Pussy said to the Owl: "You elegant fowl!
How charmingly sweet you sing!
O let us be married! Too long we have tarried:
But what shall we do for a ring?"
They sailed away, for a year and a day,
To the land where the Bong-tree grows
And there in a wood a Piggy-wig stood
With a ring at the end of his nose
His nose, His nose,
With a ring at the end of his nose.

"Dear Pig, are you willing to sell for one shilling
Your ring?" Said the Piggy, "I will."
So they took it away, and were married next day
By the Turkey who lives on the hill.
They dined on mince, and slices of quince,
Which they ate with a runcible spoon;
And hand in hand, on the edge of the sand,
They danced by the light of the moon,
The moon, The moon,
They danced by the light of the moon.

The Owl

MOLLY DE HAVAS

When night is falling in the wood
The Owl wakes up and cries "Tu-whoo!
Dear children, you must go to bed,
Your day is done, Goodnight to you.
For me the darkness is the day,
And I must hunt the whole night through
To feed my hungry owlets, till
At dawn we sleep,
Tu-whit Tu-whoo!"

To a Butterfly

WILLIAM WORDSWORTH

I've watched you now a full half-hour,
Self-poised upon that yellow flower;
And, little Butterfly! indeed
I know not if you sleep or feed.
How motionless! — not frozen seas
More motionless! and then
What joy awaits you, when the breeze
Hath found you out among the trees,
And calls you forth again!

This plot of orchard-ground is ours;
My trees they are, my Sister's flowers;
Here rest your wings when they are weary;
Here lodge as in a sanctuary!
Come often to us, fear no wrong;
Sit near us on the bough!
We'll talk of sunshine and of song,
And summer days, when we were young;
Sweet childish days, that were as long
As twenty days are now.

Busy Bees

CHRISTINA T. OWEN

It makes me feel a little dizzy
To watch the bees so small and busy
They gather pollen at all hours
To make the honey from the flowers.

High June

C.A. MORIN

Fiddle-de-dee!
Grasshoppers three,
Rollicking over the meadow;
Scarcely the grass,
Bends as they pass,
So fairy-light is their tread, O!

Said Grasshopper One,
"The summer's begun,
This sunshine is driving me crazy!"
Said Grasshopper Two,
"I feel just like you!"
And leapt to the top of a daisy.

"Please wait for me!"
Cried Grasshopper Three,
"My legs are ready for hopping!"
So grasshoppers three,
Fiddle-de-dee,
Raced all the day without stopping.

Wiggly Worm

CHRISTINA T. OWEN

It's Wiggly Wiggle-Worm come up on top
To squirm and wiggle; he just won't stop.
He'll stretch and stretch, and crawl and crawl,
See — first he's big, and then he's small.
It's Wiggly Wiggle-worm come to call.

Sir Miriapod

OLIN WANNAMAKER

Sir Miriapod, the centipede,
While strolling down the road,
With shoes on all his hundred feet,
Met Bufonid, the toad.

"Why Toad," said he in lofty scorn,
"I wonder how you do
With only four feet to your name
And not a single shoe!"

But, when Sir Miriapod did gaze
On his own hundred shoes,
His foolish, self-conceited thoughts
Did all his legs confuse.
He could not run, he could not walk,
He could not even crawl!
But, while the carefree Toad hopped on,
There he did squirm and sprawl!
Now you may sympathise with him,
But I do not at all!

The Snail

WILLIAM COWPER

To grass, or leaf, or fruit, or wall,
The snail sticks close, nor fears to fall,
As if he grew there, house and all
        Together.

Within that house secure he hides,
When danger imminent betides
Of storms, or other harm besides
        Of weather.

Give but his horns the slightest touch,
His self-collecting power is such
He shrinks into his house with much
        Displeasure.

Where'er he dwells, he dwells alone,
Except himself has chattels none,
Well satisfied to be his own
        Whole treasure.

Thus hermit-like, his life he leads,
Nor partner of his banquet needs,
And if he meets one only feeds
        The faster.

Who seeks him must be worse than blind
(He and his house are so combined)
If, finding it, he fails to find
        Its master.

The Tadpole

ELIZABETH GOULD

Underneath the water-weeds
Small and black, I wriggle,
And life is most surprising!
Wiggle! waggle! wiggle!

There's every now and then a most
Exciting change in me,
I wonder, wiggle! waggle!
What I SHALL turn out to be!

The Frog

ROSE FYLEMAN

A little green frog once lived in a pool,
The sun was hot but the water was cool;
He sat in the pool the whole day long,
And sang a queer little, dear little song.

"Quaggery do, quaggery dee,
No one was ever so happy as me."
He sang this song to his little green brother,
And if you don't mind it then make me another.

Toad the Tailor

M.E. HUSSEY

Toad the Tailor lived in a well,
    Croak, croak, croak he would sing.
Instead of a knocker his door had a bell,
    Croak! C-C-C-Croak!
The bell it was hung with the greatest of care,
    Croak, croak, croak he would sing.

At the top of the steps leading down to him there,
    Croak! croak, croak he would sing.
By the light of a lantern his customers came,
    Croak, croak, croak he would sing.
He measured them all by the length of their name,
    Croak, croak, croak he would sing.
But nobody grumbled a bit about that,
    Croak, croak, croak he would sing.
It suited the thin and it suited the fat,
    Croak, croak, croak he would sing.
In time the old Toad grew as rich as could be,
    Croak, croak, croak he would sing.
So he hung out a notice, "All tailoring Free,"
    Croak! C-C-C-Croak.

Earth Folk

WALTER DE LA MARE

The cat she walks on padded claws,
The wolf on the hills lays stealthy paws,
Feathered birds in the rain-sweet sky
At their ease in the air, flit low, flit high.

The oak's blind, tender roots pierce deep,
His green crest towers, dimmed in sleep,
Under the stars whose thrones are set
Where never prince hath journeyed yet.

Who's In?

ELIZABETH FLEMING

"The door is shut fast
    And everyone's out."
"But people don't know
    What they're talking about!"
Say the fly on the wall,
And the flame on the coals,
And the dog on his rug,
And the mice in their holes,
And the kitten curled up,
And the spiders that spin —
"What, everyone out?
    Why, everyone's in!"

Zoo Manners

EILEEN MATHIAS

Be careful what you say or do
When you visit the animals at the Zoo.
    Don't make fun of the Camel's hump —
    He's very proud of his noble bump.
Don't laugh too much at the Chimpanzee —
He thinks he's as wise as you or me.
    And the Penguins strutting round the lake
    Can understand remarks you make.
Treat them as well as they do you,
And you'll always be welcome at the Zoo.

Unstooping

WALTER DE LA MARE

Low on his fours the Lion
    Treads with the surly Bear;
But Men straight upward from the dust
    Walk with their heads in air;
The free sweet winds of heaven,
    The sunlight from on high
Beat on their clear bright cheeks and brows
    As they go striding by;
The doors of all their houses
    They arch so they may go,
Uplifted o'er the four-foot beasts,
    Unstooping, to and fro.

Farming and Building

Farming

MARGARET MORGAN

To dig the ditch,
To plough the land,
To this the farmer
Turns his hand.

To sow the seed,
To hoe and weed,
To give the plants
The light they need.

To milk the cows,
To feed the hens,
To clean the pigs
Within their pens.

To cut the corn,
To store the grain,
To bring the sheep
To be sheared again.

To care for the soil,
To let it rest,
To feed it — so
It gives its best.

To grow good food
For beast and man;
The farmer works
As best he can.

A Growing Rhyme

WESTRUP

A farmer once planted some little brown seeds
With a pit a pit, pit a pat, pit a pat, pat.
He watered them often and pulled up the weeds,
With a tug-tug at this, and a tug-tug at that.
The little seeds grew tall and green in the sun,
With a push-push up here, and a push-push up there,
And a beautiful plant grew from everyone,
With a hey-diddle, holding their heads in the air.

The Shrewmouse

FIONA MACLEOD

The creatures with the shining eyes
    That live among the tender grass
See great stars falling down the skies
    And mighty comets pass.

Torches of thought within the mind
    Wave fire upon the dancing streams
Of souls that shake upon them wind
    In rain of falling dreams.

The shrewmouse builds her windy nest
    And laughs amid the corn:
She hath no dreams within her breast:
    God smiled when she was born.

The Seed Shop

MURIEL STEWART

Here in a quiet and dusty room they lie,
Faded as crumbled stone or shifting sand,
Forlorn as ashes, shrivelled, scentless, dry,
Meadows and gardens running through my hand.
In this brown husk, a dale of hawthorn dreams,
A cedar in this narrow cell is thrust.
It will drink deeply of a century's streams.
These lilies will make summer on my dust,
Here in their safe and simple house of death,
Sealed in their shells, a million roses leap.
Here I can blow a garden with my breath
And in my hand a forest lies asleep.

The Scarecrow

MICHAEL FRANKLIN

A scarecrow stood in a field one day,
    Stuffed with straw,
    Stuffed with hay;
He watched the folk on the king's highway,
    But never a word said he.

Much he saw, but naught did heed,
    Knowing not night,
    Knowing not day,
For, having naught, did nothing heed,
    And never a word said he.

A little grey mouse had made its nest,
    Oh so wee,
    Oh so grey,
In a sleeve of a coat that was poor Tom's best,
    But the scarecrow naught said he.

His hat was the home of a small jenny wren,
    Ever so sweet,
    Ever so gay;
A squirrel had put by his fear of men,
    And kissed him, but naught heeded he.

Ragged old man, I loved him well,
    Stuffed with straw,
    Stuffed with hay;
Many's the tale that he could tell,
    But never a word says he.

The House that Jack Built

TRADITIONAL

This is the farmer sowing his corn
Who kept the cock that crowed in the morn
That woke the priest all shaven and shorn
Who married the man all tattered and torn
Who kissed the maiden all forlorn
Who milked the cow with the crumpled horn
That tossed the dog
That worried the cat
That killed the rat
That ate the malt
That lay in the house that Jack built.

Building

TREVOR SMITH WESTGARTH

To build a house that stands for years to come
We must apply our skills, but one by one.
To lay foundations deep: they must be strong
To take the weight of walls the length along.

With stretcher next to stretcher on we go —
Then header next to header in every second row,
The spirit level, too, must lie and wait
For us to check and see that walls are straight.

To keep the moisture out we must make sure
To set the damp proof course before we build much more;
Then, one by one, the bricks are laid in rows
In English Bond our little building grows.

It's almost finished now — we look with smiles
As timber strong support the roofing tiles
Which hang in rows from timbered base to top,
And last of all we fit the chimney pot.

When everyone has worked as best he can
The building will take shape more like the plan
Which, by some master architect thought out,
We built, and know what building's all about.

❖

Numbers

❖

Ten Little Dicky-Birds

TRADITIONAL

One little dicky-bird
Hopped on my shoe
Along came another one
And that made two.
Fly to the tree tops
Fly to the ground
Fly little dicky-birds
Round and round.

Two little dicky-birds
Singing in a tree
Along came another one
And that made three.
Fly to the tree tops ...

Three little dicky birds
Came to my door ...

Four ... Perched on a hive
Five ... Nesting in the ricks
Six ... Flying up to heaven
Seven ... Sat upon a gate
Eight ... Swinging on a line
Nine ... Looking at a hen ...

TRADITIONAL

One, two, buckle my shoe;
Three, four, knock at the door.
Five, six, pick up sticks,
Seven, eight, lay them straight.
Nine, ten, a big fat hen;
Eleven, twelve, dig and delve.

Dancing on the shore

TRADITIONAL

Ten little children
Dancing on the shore.
The queen waved a royal wand
And out went four.

Six little children
Dancing merrily;
The queen waved a royal wand
And out went three.

Three little children
Danced as children do;
The queen waved a royal wand
And out went two.

One little maiden
Dancing just for fun;
The queen waved a royal wand
And out went one.

Green Grow the Rushes, Ho!

TRADITIONAL

I'll sing you one, ho!
    Green grow the rushes, ho!
What is your one ho?
One is one and all alone and ever more shall be so.

I'll sing you two, ho!
    Green grow the rushes, ho!
What is your two ho?
Two, two the lily white boys, clothed all in green O
One is one and all alone and ever more shall be so.

    Three, three the rivals
    Four for the gospel makers
    Five for the symbols at your door
    Six for the six proud walkers
    Seven for the seven stars in the sky
    Eight for the April rainers
    Nine for the nine bright shiners
    Ten for the ten commandments
    Eleven for the eleven who went to heaven
    Twelve for the twelve apostles.

Counting Game

MOLLY DE HAVAS

One, two, three, four, five, six, seven,
    In my head count windows seven.
One, two, three, four, five, six,
    Point each way, that makes six.
One, two, three, four, five,
    See my fingers five.
One, two, three, four — Limbs I have four.
One, two, three — Earth, air, sea.
One, two — Me, you.
One — Done!

The Melon

CLIFFORD MONKS

The melon was one so I took my knife
And slowly cut it through
And what was one and all complete
Before us lay in two.

I cut again, 'twas plain to see
What had been two appeared as three.
I cut again, and then once more
And then I cut again
Until I saw before my eyes
The number of pieces was ten.
I cut again, again, again,
And then I saw before my eyes
The pieces were twenty-four.

The melon was one, the world is one
The facts are plain to see,
That in and about us all the world
Proceeds from unity.

ANONYMOUS

One busy housewife sweeping up the floor
Two busy housewives polishing the door
Three busy housewives washing baby's socks
Four busy housewives winding up the clocks
Five busy housewives washing out the broom
Six busy housewives tidying the room
Seven busy housewives cleaning out the sink
Eight busy housewives giving puss a drink
Nine busy housewives stirring up the stew
Ten busy housewives with nothing else to do.

Roman Figures

X shall stand for playmates TEN
V for FIVE stout stalwart men;
I for ONE, as I'm alive;
C for a HUNDRED, and D for FIVE;
M for a THOUSAND soldiers true,
and L for FIFTY, I'll tell you.

Number Poem

Through stars above, through stones below,
Through beasts, birds, flowers, even snow
Through Man and everything around him
In heavenly music they're resounding
Numbers! Numbers everywhere
Hiding here and hiding there.
One is Man, and one the world
Two the sun and moon,
Three are waking, dream and sleep
And four the seasons through.
Five the sepals of the rose
Six was Gabriel's star,
Seven days are in each week
And seven the planets are.

For Class One

CLAIRE DUBROVIC

We can count, and we can write,
We can knit and we can fight,
We can listen and recite
English, French and German too,
But wait until we're in class two!

Arithmetic Verses

ANONYMOUS

There was a family strange indeed;
Each member had a peculiar speed.
They could walk for half a day
Counting footsteps all the way.
Here they come,
Number one.

1. I am proper, neat and prim
My walk is straight, my clothes are trim
So I count my steps and you will see
That every one's the same for me.
One, two, three, four, five, six,
seven, eight, nine, ten, eleven, twelve

2. But *my* two steps are *not* the *same.*
For I must lean upon my cane.
Although I'm bent and weak and old
I can still count with numbers bold.
One, *two,* three, *four,* five, *six,*
seven, *eight,* nine, *ten,* eleven, *twelve.*

3. I'm a *lad,* light and *gay*
And I'd *much* rather *play.*
I can *run* with my *ball*
While the *numbers* I call.
One, two, *three,* four, five, *six,*
seven, eight, *nine,* ten, eleven, *twelve.*

4. My step is *strong*
I'll not go *wrong*
With all my *might*
I'll guard what's *right.*
I'll always *know*
How far to *go.*
One, two, three, *four,* five, six,
seven, *eight,* nine, ten, eleven, *twelve.*

5. Like a mouse I *go*
Fearfully tip-*toe*
Looking to the *left,*
Looking to the *right;*
Watching to and *fro*
Danger's not in *sight.*
Lightly I ar*rive,*
I am number *five.*
    One, two, three, four, *five,*
    six, seven, eight, nine, *ten.*

6. One, two, three, four, five, *six*
I can do lots of *tricks!*
I've a friend — number *three* —
He's a helper to *me.*
He has taught me to *play*
But I have my own *way.*
    One, two, three, four, five, *six,*
    seven, eight, nine, ten, eleven, *twelve.*

10. A giant am I, just sauntering by
To numbers so high I quickly will fly.
    Ten, twenty, thirty, forty, fifty,
    sixty, seventy, eighty, ninety, a hundred.

Making Tens

How many ways can you bring me ten?
Now think fast, my merry little men.
Glad to be first, see Jack's eyes shine
As he quickly comes to me with one and —

The Number Twelve

ANONYMOUS

Twelve children together are we
Merry and bright as you can see,
Twelve children hand in hand
In one circle here we stand.

Each with a partner, hand in hand,
Six pairs now before us stand.
TWELVE IS SIX LOTS OF TWO.

Into two rings now we run
Six in each ring, quickly done.
TWELVE IS TWO LOTS OF SIX.

Into four rings now we run
Three in each ring, quickly done.
TWELVE IS FOUR LOTS OF THREE.

Wait and we will show you more:
Three rings now, in each is four.
TWELVE IS THREE LOTS OF FOUR.

[*Then all the children dance back into the circle again and skip round chanting the first verse*]

Number Poem

ANONYMOUS

The bright-eyed stars do in the number rest
And every man is by the numbers blest:
By one when upright on the earth he stands,
By two when lovingly he lifts his hands,
By three when he awakes, or dreams, or sleeps,
By four when every year its seasons keeps,
By five when opens out the summer's rose,
By six when Gabriel's snow-white lily blows,
By seven when every week its days do bring,
Thus do the numbers through the great world ring.

For Tidying Away

CLAIRE DUBROVIC

One, two, three, four, five, six, seven,
All books closed before eleven.
Eight, nine, ten, eleven, twelve —
And now put them on the shelf.

A Mathematics Poem

MICHAEL MOTTERAM

A circle has lots of possibilities;
There are many directions to go.
But with a line that is straight —
There can only be this way or that!
If you live from the centre of a circle
you will find your life all about you.
But should you live on a railway track
you can only go forward or back!

Time Rhyme

DOROTHY HARRER

Sixty seconds make a minute,
Put a lot of kindness in it.
Sixty minutes make an hour.
Work with all your might and power.
Twelve bright hours make a day,
Time enough for work and play.
Twelve dark hours through the night
Give us sleep till morning light.
Seven days a week will make.
This we'll learn if pains we take.
Four to five weeks make the months.
Remember this or be a dunce.
Twelve long months will make a year,
In one of them your birthday, dear.

– – – ❖ – – –

Tongue Twisters

– – – ❖ – – –

Three crooked cripples went through Cripplegate
And through Cripplegate went three crooked cripples.

Three grey geese in a green field grazing
Grey were the geese and green was the grazing.

A flea and a fly in a flue
Were imprisoned, so what could they do?
Said the fly let us flee,
Said the flea let us fly,
So they flew through a flaw in the flue.

Higglety, pigglety, pop!
The dog has eaten the mop;
The cat's in a flurry,
The pig's in a hurry,
Higglety, pigglety, pop!

Hoddley, poddley, puddle and frogs,
Cats are to marry the poodle dogs;
Cats in blue jackets, and dogs in red hats,
What will become of the mice and rats?

There's no need to light a night-light
On a light night like tonight
For a night-light's a slight light
On a light night like tonight.

Peter Piper picked a peck of pickled pepper.
Did Peter Piper pick a peck of pickled pepper?
If Peter Piper picked a peck of pickled pepper,
Where's the peck of pickled pepper Peter Piper picked?

Swan swam over the sea
Swim, swan, swim!
Swan swam back again
Well swum, swan!

She sells sea shells on the sea shore.
The shells she sells are sea shells I'm sure
If she sells sea shells on the sea shore,
Where are the Seashore shells she sells?

Swing, swing, and sing as we swing
Our voice will ring
If we sing as we swing.

Splish! splosh! splish! splosh!
Through the puddles Tim is splashing
Splish! splosh! splish! splosh!
Soon his clothes will need a washing.

Timothy Titus took two tees
To tie two tubs to two tall trees
To terrify terrible Thomas a Tattermus

Alphabet Tongue Twisters

ANONYMOUS

A Andrew Airpump asked his Aunt her Ailment:
Did Andrew Airpump ask his Aunt her Ailment?
B Billy Button bought a buttered biscuit
Did Billy Button buy a buttered biscuit?
C Captain Crackskull cracked a catchpole's cockscomb.
Did ...
D Davy Dolldrum dreamed he drove a dragon.
E Eddie Elkrig ate an empty eggshell.
F Francis Fribble found a Frenchman's filly.
G Gaffer Gilpine got a goose and gander.
H Humphrey Huckleback had a hundred hedgehogs.
I Inigo Impey itched for an Indian image.
J Jumping Jacky jeered at a jesting juggler.
K Kimbo Kemble kicked his kinsman's kettle.
L Larry Lawrence lost his lass and lobster.
M Manhew Mendlegs missed his magic marker.
N Neddy Noodle nipped his neighbour's nutmegs.
O Olive Oglethorpe ogled an owl and oyster.
P Peter Piper picked a peck of pickled pepper.
Q Quixote Quicksight quizzed a queerish quidbox.
R Roland Rumpus rode a raw-boned racer.
S Sammy Smellie smelled a smell of smelting.
T Tip-Top Tommy turned a Turk for twopence.
U Uncle's Usher urged an ugly urchin.
V Villy Veedon viped his vig and vaistcoat
W Walter Wiggler won a walking wager.

XYZ Have made my brains to crack-o,
X smokes, Y snuffs, and Z chews strong tobacco;
Yet often by XYZ much learning's taught;
But Peter Piper beats them all to nought.

Moses

Moses supposes his toeses are roses,
But Moses supposes erroneously;
For nobody's toeses are posies of roses
As Moses supposes his toeses to be.

The Tutor

A tutor who taught on the flute,
Tried to teach two young tooters to toot.
Said the two to the tutor:
"Is it harder to toot
Or to tutor two tooters to toot?"

– – – ❖ – – –

Grammar

– – – ❖ – – –

The Alphabet

Alphabet

TRADITIONAL

A B C D E F G
Little Robin Redbreast sitting on a tree;
H I J K L M N
He made love to little Jenny Wren;
O P Q R S T U
Dear little Jenny, I want to marry you.
V and W, X Y Z
Poor little Jenny she blushed quite red.

Alphabet

MARGARET MORGAN

A is for Angel with heavenly wings;
B is for Bird that beautifully sings;
C is for Cat, curled up by the fire;
D is for Dog Rose — sometimes called briar;
E is for Eagle that soars in the sky;
F is for Flag, fluttering on high;
G is for Giraffe who looks over the wall;
H is for Hamster, so furry and small;
I is for Iceberg that floats in the sea;
J is for Jungle where animals roam free;
K is for Kingfisher, seen by the lake;
L is for Lamp that in darkness we take;
M is for Moon to shine in the night;
N is for Note that we hastily write;
O is for Orange so juicy and sweet;
P is for Peacock — not seen in the street;
Q is for Queen with jewels and crown;
R is for Rabbit, all fluffy and brown;
S is for Sea and for Sun and for Sand;
T is for Trumpet that plays in the Band;
U is for Unicorn, seen long ago;
V is for Valley that dips deep and low;
W is for Well — where Wishes are made;
X is for eXciting games that are played;
Y is for Yacht that sails on the sea;
Z is for Zoo — where Zebras may be.

This is the Alphabet
A through to Z.

26 letters — and each
Has been said.

Parts of Speech

Names

CLAIRE DUBROVIC

If the names of things you'd know
Don't ask verbs; to nouns you must go!

Nouns

Mountain, hill and stone and rock
House and castle, ship and dock,
Lion, tiger, camel, horse,
Tulip, lily, nettle, gorse,
Thought, consideration, word and deed,
Love and kindness, help in need.

We've heard their names, what do they do?

Verbs

They lie and sleep, they do not wake.
Men plough and build, they cook and bake.
They feed and blossom, die and grow.
They roar and gallop, snort and blow.
They think and plan, they work and play.
They laugh and cry, they hope and pray.

Their names we know and what they do,
What are they like, we're asking you?

Adjectives

White and black and green and blue
Fragrant, prickly, dainty or tall,
Wild or gentle, big or small.
Beautiful, ugly, old or new
Gentle, helpful, friendly ever,
Cruel, unkind, grumpy never.

Verb and noun and adjective
Understanding of the world they give.

Punctuation Verses

DOROTHY HARRER

I am the full stop. I love to rest.
All sentences stop at my request.

Whoopee! Hooray!
Look out! Make way!
I'm here! I'm there! And everywhere!
Whatever the excitement rare,
The exclamation mark is there!

I want to know
What is your name?
Where do you live?
What is your fame?
What answer will you give?
The question-mark am I,
And can you tell me why?

When the sentences are long,
Running ever on and on,
I run with them, so nimble and merry,
To give you a breathing space,
Lest you grow weary.
I am the comma, so nimble and busy.
Without me the sentences might make you dizzy.

The Parts of Speech

VIRGINIA FIELD BIRDSALL

The Verb
I am a verb, I like to act,
To walk, to run, to dance — it's a fact.
To plough, to build, to work, to strive,
I like to feel that I'm alive!
But sometimes I just say, "I am,"
And act as meek as a little lamb.

The Noun
I am a noun; I give names to things,
To persons, from beggars to royal kings;
To animals also, great and small,
To flowers, and trees that grow so tall.
To things like tables and chairs and sticks,
To houses and stones, concrete and bricks;
And to things you can't see or hear or feel,
Like goodness and truth, honour and zeal!
I like to be quiet — I don't run about —
I just sit still and let others shout.

The Pronoun
I am a pronoun; it isn't quite fair —
I'm only about when the noun isn't there!
Sometimes I'm *I* and sometimes I'm *you,*
Or *he, she,* or *it,* or *they* or *them,* too;
I change my form when it suits my whim,
Then *she* becomes *her* and *he* becomes *him.*

The Adjectives
We are the adjectives — artists too —
We stick to the nouns as your skin sticks to you.
I call the man *great* or *good* or *bad.*
I call the beast *large* or *fierce* or *sad.*
I can paint the grass *green* and the flowers all *gay.*
We dance through the world in our *colourful* way.

The Adverbs
We are the adverbs! We've lots of fun
Telling *how, when* or *where* the action is done;
Whether *neatly,* or *carelessly, promptly* or not,
We have you children right on the spot.
You act *bravely* and *honestly, wisely* and *well,*
Or *falsely* and *foolishly,* adverbs will tell.
Either *now* or *later* or *sometime* or *never,*
Immediately, presently, soon or *forever,*
Either *here* or *there* or *somewhere around,*
Along with the verb the adverb is found.
But sometimes we go with the adjectives too,
When the sun's *very* bright and the sky's *very* blue.
Or with other adverbs we sometimes wait,
When you walk *very* slowly and come *very* late.

The Preposition
A preposition small am I,
But others are not half so spry!
I'm *up* the mountain, *down* the glen,
Through the city, *among* the men,
Under the river, *over* the sea,
Or *up in* the tree-tops! There you'll find me.
I'm *with* and *of* and *from* and *by,*
Pointing always, low or high.

The Conjunction
I am the word that joins — conjunction;
I have a plain but useful function.
What would you do without your *and?*
Your *or?* Your *if?* I'm in demand,
Because, unless your work you do,
You're negligent and lazy too!

The Articles
The articles small are we;
We like to make ourselves known;
Fat *A, an* and *the* — but not one of us three >>

Can stand for a minute alone.
Three small articles are we
And we keep nouns company.

The Interjection
I'm the interjection wild,
Dear to almost every child
Oh, how lovely! *Ouch,* take care!
Alas! Hurrah! Hello! Beware!
Oh, how noble! *Look,* red light!
My, you gave me such a fright!

Parts of Speech

TREVOR SMITH WESTGARTH

A Noun Is — a Verb Does

A noun's a clown
A saint, a frown
A dog or cat
Or something that
Is.

A verb walks
Or slips and talks
Or hits and pats
Names any action that's
Doing!

Pronoun
If you do not wish
To name a name
Again and again
And again the same
To use a pronoun you might try
Like *his* or *hers* or *its* or *my,*
Or *they* or *her* or *him* or *we,*

Ours or *theirs* or *I* or *me,*
This or *that* or *these* or *thine,*
Those, himself, herself or *mine.*

Adjective

An adjective describes
That something's *blue,*
Or *red* or *great* or *poor* or *new,*
Or *smooth* or *rough* or *dark* or *light,*
It always tells what things are like.

Adverbs

Adverbs add to the verb to tell *how, when* or *where,*
They give a better picture, and information share.
Adverbs like *yesterday, immediately* and *then*
All help us to understand a little more of *"When?"*
Adverbs like *away, outside, above* and *there*
Answer the question if you ask it *"Where?"*
Adverbs like *quickly, clumsily* or *wisely*
Describe the manner in which a thing is done precisely.

Prepositions

Prepositions gently guide us;
Running through or falling down,
Prepositions help describe us,
As black as soot, of great renown.
Prepositions stand beside us;
Steak with chips, a house in town,
So prepositions are friends to all,
The bridge to adjective, verb or noun.

The Four Sentences

DOROTHY HARRER

Commands
Listen to the night wind blow.
See the swirling flakes of snow.
Close the window. Shut the door.
Keep out the wild wind's angry roar.
Light the fire. Let it blaze.
Warm the house with its hot rays.

Exclamations
How wonderful the morning is!
Oh, what a sparkling day!
Sky's blue around the golden sun!
The wind has died away!

Statements
The golden sun shines on the snow.
The trees blue shadows make.
The colours of God's own rainbow
Twinkle in each snowflake.

Questions
Where do snowflakes come from?
Why are they so white?
Who gives them each a separate form?
How far has been their flight?
And what creates the rainbow
In each white star of snow?

Verbs

ANONYMOUS

Frogs jump.
Caterpillars hump.
Worms wiggle.
Beetles jiggle.
Rabbits hop.
Horses clop.
Snakes slide.
Seagulls glide.
Mice creep.
Deer leap.
Foxes prowl.
Dogs growl.
Puppies bounce.
Kittens pounce.
Lions stalk.
I walk.

EILEEN HUTCHINS

The sun says "I glow,"
The wind says "I blow,"
The stream says "I flow,"
The plant says "I grow,"
And man says "I know."

Punctuate

TRADITIONAL

Every lady in this land
Has twenty nails upon each hand
Five and twenty on hands and feet
All this is true without deceit.

Construe

ANONYMOUS

Infir taris,
In oak noneis,
Inmud eelsare,
Inclay noneare.
Goatseativy
Mareseatoats.

Spelling Verse

TREVOR SMITH WESTGARTH

William was a worrier
Inquisitive and wild.
Wanting to always know more
Than any other child,
Whining and requesting,
And insisting that he knew
Why and what and wherefore
And whether, when and who,
And whose was which while which was whose
And what was where and when,
And when anybody told him
He would ask the whole thing again.

Submitted to a Professor of Literature

BY A FOREIGN STUDENT

The wind was rough
And cold and blough
She kept her hands inside her mough.

It chilled her through
Her nose turned blough
And still the squall the faster flough.

And yet although
There was no snough
The weather was a cruel fough.

It made her cough
(Pleease do not scough)
She coughed until her hat blew ough.

Vowels

Verses with Vowels

Ay Awake! Awake! and take your way, be brave and gay today!
E Easily sweep the eagles free, each to his eyrie at evening.
O Sow the oats and mow the oats and sow the rosy clover.
U Soon through the blue gloom the cool moon will move
Ah No harm can alarm my ardent heart, fast guarded with calm.

We say "ah" to all wonderful things that are.
The rainbow arch and the watching star.
When day departs a single star
Marks how bright the heavens are.
See afar the moon embark
Upon the ocean of the dark.

Guarded from harm
Cared for by Angels
Stand we here
Loving and strong
Truthful and good.

In my garden stands a tree
Stands as straight as straight can be.
Roots and branches spreading far
On the branches apples are.
Hats and bags wide open hold
Golden apples to enfold.

Ah When day departs, a single star
Marks how bright the heavens are.
See afar, the moon embark
Upon the ocean of the dark.

O Alone upon a throne of gold,
With robes of purple fold on fold,
The Monarch, lord of lands untold
Ruled his folk in days of old.

E See the dreary winter breeze
Blow the leaves from off the trees,
Sweep them down the windy street
Feel them underneath your feet!
I see, I feel, I gladly greet
The earth beneath my eager feet.

I The light that shines in heaven high,
Likes to weave the colours bright,
Sheds its kindness from the sky,
Gives us life, and might, and sight.
A little of the light am I
Like a candle in the night.

OW Our stout brown trout
Swims in and out.

O Old Mouldy the half-blind mole
Lies snugly asleep in his hole.
In black and glossy fir he's rolled
Against the cold.

E Three free sailormen we be
Here from Greenland over sea.
Here from Greenland over sea
We be breezy sailors free.

O Mr Knox keeps his socks
In a pale pink chocolate box.
Orange socks, with spots and clocks,
Oh you dandy Mr Knox.

E I see, I feel, I gradly greet
The earth beneath my eager feet.

Thoughts and Deeds

DOROTHY HARRER

Four deeds on earth can well be found
To endure, to grow,
To feel, to know,
We meet all four the whole world round.

The rocks of earth endure and bear
The weight of foot,
The grip of root,
The wash of waves and windy air.

The plants in earth do grow and wane
As seed and flower
Helped by the power
Of shining sun and splashing rain.

The beasts on earth feel love or hate;
With fang and paw
Or beak and claw
Each kind will fight for food and mate.

And man can know the world's true need
For rock and tree
And beast, and he
Can learn to do the four-fold deed.

Consonants

Rhymes for Consonants

ANONYMOUS

Peter and Michael were two little menikin,
They kept a cock and a fat little henikin;
Instead of an egg, it laid a gold penikin,
Oh, how they wish it would do it againikin!

Hey diddle dinkety, poppety pet,
The merchants of London they wear scarlet;
Silk in the collar and gold in the hem,
So merrily march with the merchantmen.

Pitty Patty Polt!
Shoe the wild colt,
    Here a nail,
    There a nail,
Pitty Patty Polt!

Water in bottles
Water in pans
Water in kettles
Water in cans —
It is always the shape
Of whatever it's in,
Bucket or kettle
Or bottle or tin.

Robins sang sweetly
In the autumn days,
"There are fruits for everyone.
Let us all give praise!"

Loudly blows the bitter blast
Binding snow flakes pouring fast,

Banks and bushes, bleak and bare,
Bending boughs, and biting air.
Growls the gale in gloomy glee,
Tempest tossed the tender tree
Hurling helpless leaves on high,
Swelling seas to see the sky,
Fast the foamy feathers fly.

Willie boy, Willie boy, where are you going?
  I will go with you if I may
I'm going to the meadows to see them mowing
  I'm going to see them make the hay.

Sunny Day

MOLLY DE HAVAS

A bat and a ball we will bring to the beach,
And boats to be sailed on the breezy blue bay.
We'll picnic and bathe by the big bare black rocks,
And bask in the sun of this beautiful day.

Goblin Gold

MOLLY DE HAVAS

Digging down in deepest dark and danger
Gleeful goblins gather glittering gold.
High and hard a hundred heavy hammers
Clang and clash in columned caverns cold.

Little lamps their lengthy labours lighten
Shuddering shadows show, and shifting shine.
So they ceaseless search for silver secrets,
Midget men amid the mountain mine.

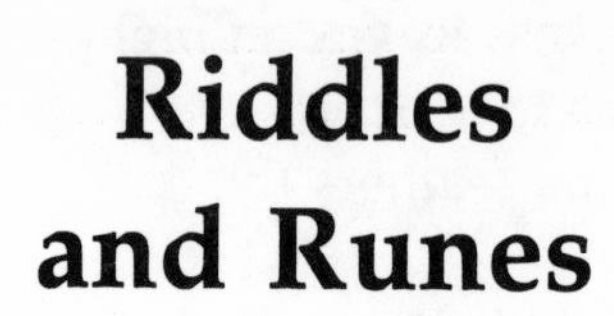

Riddles and Runes

JONATHAN SWIFT

We are very little creatures,
All of different voice and features;
One of us in glass is set,
One of us you'll find in jet.
T'other you may see in tin,
And the fourth a box within.
It can never fly from you.
[*A E I O U*]

A shoemaker makes shoes without leather
With all the four elements put together.
Fire and water, earth and air;
Every customer takes two pair.
[*A horseshoe*]

It's in the rock, but not in the stone;
It's in the marrow, but not in the bone;
It's not in the living, nor yet in the dead.
[*The letter R*]

Ten fish I caught without an eye
And nine without a tail
Six had no head, and half of eight
I weighed upon the scale.
Now who can tell me as I ask it
How many fish were in my basket?
[*None*]

Born with one name and given another,
One like, one unlike, the name of my brother.
What are my names?
[*My own names*]

The beginning of eternity,
The end of time and space,
The beginning of every end
And the end of every place.
[*The letter E*]

As round as a pear
As deep as a pail
It never cries out
Till it's caught by the tail.
[*A bell*]

What can go through water and yet
Not ever become the least bit wet?
[*Sunshine*]

Fire won't burn me, water won't drown me
Wherever I am it's cold all around me.
[*Ice*]

If Dick's father is John's son,
What relation is Dick to John?
[*Grandson*]

Brothers and sisters have I none,
But that man's father is my father's son.
[*My son*]

It isn't my sister or my brother,
But still it's the child of my father and mother
Who is it?
[*Myself*]

What have you that a pin has too?
And no doubt about it you're both worse without it!
[*Head*]

What never asks any questions at all
Yet is often answered by short and tall?
[*Telephone*]

Tell me now, what is it that
Is over your head and under your hat?
[*Hair*]

What won't go up the chimney up,
But will go up the chimney down?
What won't go down the chimney up,
But will go down the chimney down?
[*An umbrella*]

There is a thing that nothing is,
And yet it has a name.
It's sometimes tall and sometimes short,
It joins our walk, it joins our sport
And plays at every game.
[*A shadow*]

Little Nancy Etticoat
In a white petticoat
And a red nose;
The longer she stands,
The shorter she grows.
[*A lighted candle*]

From house to house he goes,
A messenger small and light;
And whether it rains or snows
He sleeps outside in the night.
[*Path*]

A man rode to town on Thursday
And stayed all night at the inn;
Then rode home upon the same Thursday —
How could such a marvel have been?
[*Horse's name was Thursday*]

What is always coming, but never arrives?
[*Tomorrow*]

Old Mother Twitchett had but one eye,
And a long tail which she let fly;
And every time she went through a gap,
A bit of her tail she left in a trap.
[*A needle*]

Runs all day and never walks
Often murmurs, never talks.
It has a bed, but never sleeps;
It has a mouth but never eats.
[*A river*]

I'm sometimes strong and sometimes weak,
But I am nobody's fool.
For there is no language I can't speak
Though I never went to school.
[*Echo*]

As I went through a field of wheat,
I picked up something good to eat.
'Twas neither fish, nor flesh, nor bone
I kept it till it walked alone.
[*An egg*]

What has four fingers and thumb
But neither flesh nor bone?
Is small, or large, or medium
Most seldom is alone.
[*A glove*]

How many balls of string would it take to reach the moon?
[*One, if it's long enough.*]

In marble wall as white as milk
Lined with a skin as soft as silk
Within a fountain crystal clear
A golden apple doth appear.
No doors there are to this stronghold
Yet thieves break in and steal the gold.
[*An egg*]

As I was going to Saint Ives,
I met a man with seven wives;
Each wife had seven sacks,
Each sack had seven cats,
Each cat had seven kits;
Kits, cats, sacks and wives,
How many going to Saint Ives?
[*One, I was*]

How do you know the difference between a sheep and a goat?
[*By looking at them.*]

Full all day, empty at rest
Both of us are very hard pressed.
[*A pair of shoes*]

'Tis in mountains, not in hills,
'Tis in meadows, not in fields,
'Tis in me and not in you,
'Tis in men and women too.
[*The letter M*]

Has 88 keys and needs no more,
But can't unlock a single door.
[*Piano*]

What's stronger than the surging ocean?
The *wind* that drives it into motion.

What is stronger than iron and steel?
They melt when the mighty *fire* they feel.

Though it's close to your eyes you'll have to admit
You never get more than a glimpse of it.
I tremble and shake at the least breath or breeze,
Yet I can take as much weight as you please.
[*Water*]

Gaelic Runes

Gaelic Poem

I bind unto myself today
The virtues of the starlit heaven
The glorious Sun's life giving ray,
The whiteness of the moon at even —
The flashing of the lightning free
The whirling wind's tempestuous shocks
The stable earth, the deep salt sea,
Around the old eternal rocks.

From *Invocation of Peace*

FIONA MACLEOD

Deep peace, pure white of the moon to you;
Deep peace, pure green of the grass to you;
Deep peace, pure brown of the earth to you;
Deep peace, pure grey of the dew to you;
Deep peace, pure blue of the sky to you!
Deep peace of the running wave to you,
Deep peace of the flowing air to you,
Deep peace of the quiet earth to you.

Gaelic Rune of Hospitality

I saw a stranger yesterday.
I put food in the eating place —
Drink in the drinking place —
Music in the listening place —
And in the blessed name of the Triune,
He blessed myself and my house,
My cattle and my dear ones
And the lark said in her song:
"Often, often, often goes
the Christ in the stranger's guise."

The Rune of St Patrick

At Tara today in this fateful hour
I place all Heaven with its power,
And the sun with its brightness,
And the snow with its whiteness,
And the fire with all the strength it hath,
And the lightning with its rapid wrath,
And the winds with their swiftness along their path,
And the sea with its deepness,
And the rocks with their steepness,
And the earth with its starkness:
    All these I place
    By God's almighty help and grace,
Between myself and the powers of darkness.

Alliteration

Betty Botter bought some butter.
"But," she said, "the butter's bitter —
If I put it in my batter
It will make my batter bitter;
But a bit of better butter
That would make my batter better."
So she bought a bit of butter
Better than her bitter butter
And she put it in her batter
And the batter was not bitter.
So 'twas better Betty Botter
Bought a bit of better butter.

Blow, breezes, blow!
Flow, rivers, flow!
Shine, sun, shine!
And grow, flowers, grow.

B is the blue of the sheltering sky
And the buds where the shielded blossoms
Build a bridge to bear the body's burden,
Brave, unbending, bold and bright.

Boys' boots are big, so when boys jump
Boys' big boots go bump, bump, bump.

Bears who look for berries early
Find bigger, better berries surely.
But bees must wait 'till buds are open
Before they buzz among the blossoms.

Billy Button bought a buttered biscuit.
Did Billy Button buy a buttered biscuit?
If Billy Button bought a buttered biscuit:
Where's the buttered biscuit Billy Button bought?

Blossoms beautiful and bright
Bursting into bloom
Bees and butterflies in flight
By the banks of broom.

C is cutting and clear and bold,
Crystal and icy, crackle and cold.

Clearly comes the curlew's cry
Scudding clouds across the sky.

Careful Katie cooked a crisp and crinkly cabbage;
Did careful Katie cook a crisp and crinkly cabbage?
If careful Katie cooked a crisp and crinkly cabbage
Where's the crisp and crinkly cabbage careful Katie cooked?

Children chiding, chaffinch chirping
Choking chimneys, cheerfully chattering.

D is a deed to be done for men
Dangerous dragon to dare in his den.

Deep in the earth when days are darkest
Dwells the summer's dawn.

Freckled fishes, flirting, flitting,
Flashing fast or floating free,
Flicking filmy fins like feathers,
Feeding from the flowing sea.

Fires are flaming,
Flickering, flashing,
Full of fury,
Full of fancy.

The farmer flings the fruitful seed
Afar upon the furrowed field.

Far in the forest on fir trees tall
Feathery snowflakes flutter and fall.

Gleeful goblins gather glittering gold.

Go, you grim and grisly bear
Growling in your gloomy lair!

Grow the grasses, cut the corn
Carry gleaning carefully.

Go! Get the guide! Guard the gate!
Gracious, good and great.

A **h**unter went a-hunting
    A-hunting for a hare,
But where he hoped the hare would be
    He found a hairy bear.
"I'm hungry," Bruno hinted,
    "I get hungry now and then."
So the hunter turned head over heels
    And hurried home again.

Hear the happy hunter's horn
High over hill and hedge and thorn.

Halt! Hold! Here!
Heaven and hell.

Jolly Jack and joyful Jill
Jumping down the jaggy hill.

K is a King, so keen and kind
Keeping the kingdom for all mankind.

Lovely colours gleaming brightly
Laughing water, lapping lightly.

Light that lingers long and low
Makes the lovely colours glow.

Merrily, merrily marches the minstrel
By meadow and marsh, over mountain and moorland.
Men are amazed by the magical music
Of marvellous melodies made by the minstrel.

Mumble and Mutter are meddlesome men
Making mistakes again and again.

Merry have we met
And merry have we been;
Merry let us part,
And merry meet again.

With a merry sing-song
Happy, gay and free,
With a merry ding-dong
Again we'll happy be.

Now the night is nigh its noon
Nimble gnomes beneath the moon.

Peerless princess proudly dancing
Tulips tall and peacocks prancing.

Pansies purple, poppies red
Primrose pale with golden head.

Peaceful be the pilgrim's purpose
Powerful his penitence.

Race to the moon, reach to the stars
Ride round the earth and rocket to Mars.

Round and round the rugged rock
The ragged rascal ran.

Rustle of leaves and ripple of rain
Roving of rivers across the plain.

Spitting and spewing,
Splitting and splattering
Spilling and spoiling,
Spellbound: the sprite.

Snow and ice and silvered hedges
Sleet and slush and slides and sledges.

Sailing ships on swelling seas
Shining sun on summer breeze.

In summer shall the shining sun
Surely bless the slender shoots.

Totally tired he tossed his turban,
Trembling like treetops
In turmoil of tempest.

Though the threat of thirst or thunder
Thin the crops or flood the wheat,
Thickly thrive the thorny thistles
Through the wet and through the heat.

Thirty thousand thoughtless boys
Thought they'd make a thundering noise;
So with thirty thousand thumbs,
They thumped on thirty thousand drums.

Through the thick and thorny thistles
Thrust and thrashed the thirsty throstles.

The **V**apours have vanished
That vaguely veiled my view.
Vivid, virtuous, vast and void.
Never be victim of villainous vices.

Walter Wiggler won a walking wager.
Did Walter Wiggler win a walking wager?
If Walter Wiggler won a walking wager
Where is Walter Wiggler who won a walking wager?

Over wintry wind-whipped waves
The white-winged seagulls wildly sweep;
Weaving, winding, wheeling, whistling,
Where the wide waste waters weep.

Watchful we will walk together,
Wander wide in wintry weather.

Whether the weather be cold,
Or whether the weather be hot;
Whether the weather be fine,
Or whether the weather be not;
Whatever the weather
We'll weather the weather,
Whether we like it or not!

From *Inversnaid*

GERALD MANLEY HOPKINS

What would the world be once bereft
Of wet and of wildness? Let them be left,
O let them be left, wildness and wet;
Long live the weeds and the wilderness yet.

Miss T

ANONYMOUS

It's a very odd thing
As odd as can be —
Whatever Miss T eats
Turns into Miss T;
Porridge and apples,
Mince, muffins, and mutton,
Jam, junket, jumbles —
Not a rap, not a button
It matters; the moment
They're out of her plate,
Though shared by Miss Butcher
And sour Mr Bate;
Tiny and cheerful
And neat as can be
Whatever Miss T eats
Turns into Miss T.

The Forging of the Sword by Fire

From *Siegfried*

RICHARD WAGNER

Needful, needful masterful sword
What blow was that, that broke thee.
To shreds I've shattered thy shining steel
Now flames the fire round thy fragments —
    Ho hei, ho ho, ho hei, ho ho —
    Bellows blow, brighten the glow.

Wild in woodlands waxed a tree
That I in the forest felled.
The good brown ash to charcoal I burned
On the hearth in heaps now it lies —
    Ho hei, ho ho, ho hei, ho ho —
    Bellows blow, brighten the glow.

The charcoal I made me
How bravely it burns
How fiercely it flames and glows.
In showers of sparks, it scatters its fire
Fusing the shreds of the steel.
    Ho hei, ho ho, ho hei, ho ho —
    Bellows blow, brighten the glow.

From *The Blacksmiths*

FIFTEENTH CENTURY ENGLISH POEM

Swart, smerched smiths smattered with smoke,
Drive me to death with the din of their dents,
Such noise on nights ne'er heard man never.
Such clashing of cries and clattering of knocks.
The craftsmen clamour for coal, coal, coal!
And blow their bellows their brains to burst.

They jostle and jangle, they jape and they jest
They groove and they grind and they grumble together,
Hot with the heaving of heated hammers.
Of thick bulls hide are their branded aprons,
Their shanks are shod 'gainst shooting sparks.

Huge hammers they have and hard to handle
Stark strokes strike they on the steeled stock
"Well wrought, well wrought, well wrought,"
Might daunt the devil
Such life they lead,
All armourers, founders, forgemen,
Christ save them!

ANONYMOUS

Forge me with fire a sword for my smiting
Fright to my foes and flame to my fighting.
Shape me a shield both forceful and fierce,
Stalwart and shapely to fend against fear.
Strike me a spear to speed as a shaft,
Fearless to fly as a shot from the start.
Staunch be my front against fury assailed,
Strong be my soul where the feeble have failed.

Blacksmith Pain

OTTO BURBAUM

Pain is a blacksmith
Hard is his hammer.
With flying flames
His hearth is hot:
A straining storm
Of forces fierce
Blows his bellows.
Heats his hammers

And these he tempers
With blows tremendous
Till hard they hold —
Well, well, forges pain,
No storm destroys
No frost consumes
No rust corrodes
What pain has forged.

– – – ❖ – – –

The Elements and Nature Spirits

– – – ❖ – – –

ALFRED CECIL HARWOOD

The sun is in my heart
He warms me with his power,
And wakens life and love,
In bird and beast and flower.

The stars above my head
Are shining in my mind,
As spirits of the world
That in my thoughts I find.

The earth whereon I tread
Lets not my feet go through,
But strongly doth uphold
The weight of deeds I do.

Then I must thankful be
That man on earth I dwell,
To know and love the world
And work all creatures well.

The Four Elements

ANONYMOUS

Earth

We, the stones on which you stand
Hold the waters and build the land.
In caves of darkest earth
Find we our crystal birth.
The sun with radiant light
Makes us sparkling bright
These are the gifts we hold for you
Of blood red, white, and blue.

Water

We are the waters cool and deep
That rush and run, or soundly sleep.
Down the mountain, through the lake
To the sea our path we make
Under moon and stars afloat
Across the waves we'll bear your boat,
We are the waters cool and deep
That rush and run, or soundly sleep.

Air

We are the winds that weep and wail
Blow a breeze and swell the sail
And wear a cloak of wonder rare
Of silver, gold and stars that stare.
And joy we spin in every fold
Our gift on earth for you to hold.
We are the winds that weep and wail
Blow a breeze and swell the sail.

Fire

We, the bright red fiery flames
Crackle and roar, that nothing tames.
Sparks like shooting stars they fly
Helpers we are of sun on high.
With golden sword the cold we slay
And bring you warmth to cheer your stay.
We, the bright red fiery flames
Crackle and roar, that nothing tames.

Mother Earth

EILEEN HUTCHINS

Mother Earth,
Mother Earth,
Take our seed
And give it birth.

Sister Rain,
Sister Rain,
Shed thy tears
To swell the grain.

Father Sun,
Gleam and glow,
Until the roots
Begin to grow.

Brother Wind,
Breathe and blow
Then the blade
Green will grow.

Earth and Sun,
And wind and rain,
Turn to gold
The living grain.

The Growing River

RODNEY BENNETT

At first the river's very small,
And can't float anything at all;
But later as it journeys on,
It's large enough to float a swan.

It grows till it can safely float
A slim canoe and then a boat;
And later still, as like or not,
It manages to float a yacht.

And presently, when really large,
It takes a steamer, then a barge.
And last it passes busy quays
And floats great ships to foreign seas.

The River

MOLLY DE HAVAS

I spring within a moss-grown dell
    on rugged mountain land,
Where only stunted pine trees,
    shallow-rooted, sparely stand,
And slow I grow with melted snow
    from peaks on either hand.

I choose myself the quickest path
    to find my way downhill,
And all the time from every side
    new trickles swell my rill,
From sodden peat and cloudy mist
    I draw their water chill.

I ripple over pebbles,
    over waterfalls I leap,
I speed through narrow clefts where I
    must dig my channel deep,
Then through the valley meadowlands
    in placid curves I sweep.

Small fishes live within me,
    in my reeds the wildfowl nest;
Kingfisher, rat and otter
    in my banks may safely rest,
And all poor weary creatures
    are by crystal water blest.

Sometimes my sparkling clarity
    is hidden by a frown,
Of dirt and oil and rubbish
    as I pass a busy town;
And sometimes little boats I bear
    with sails of white or brown.

At last I reach a sandy shore
    whereon great waves foam,
By nature bound, yet ever free,
    I need no longer roam,
The path designed I followed
    to the sea which is my home.

The Rainbow

WALTER DE LA MARE

I saw the lovely arch
Of Rainbow span the sky,
The gold sun burning
As the rain swept by.

In bright-ringed solitude
The showery foliage shone
One lovely moment,
And the Bow was gone.

The Rainbow

MICHAEL DRUMMOND

Created through and by the rain,
Woven entirely out of light,
It shines above with body bright.
Red on the outside, a line of orange,
The yellow expands to meet the blue,
Making green between the two.
Then comes indigo, the deepest hue,
And warmer violet inside all
This bow of seven spans the heaven,
Colours, of a delicate shade,
All from light and darkness made.

The Rainbow

CHRISTINA ROSSETTI

If all were rain and never sun
No bow would span the hill.
If all were sun and never rain
There'd be no rainbow still.

The Rune of the Four Winds

FIONA MACLEOD

By the Voice in the corries
When the Polestar danceth:

By the Voice on the summits
The dead feet know:

By the soft wet cry
When the Heat-star troubleth:

By the plaining and moaning
Of the Sigh of the Rainbows:

By the four white winds of the world,
Whose father the golden Sun is,
Whose mother the wheeling Moon is,
The North and the South and the East and the West:
By the four good winds of the world,
That Man knoweth,
That One dreadeth,
That God blesseth —

Be all well
On mountain and moorland and lea,
On loch-face and lochan the river,
On shore and shallow and sea!

By the Voice of the Hollow
Where the worm dwelleth:

By the Voice of the Hollow
Where the sea-wave stirs not:

By the Voice of the Hollow
That sun hath not seen yet:

By the three dark winds of the world;
The chill dull breath of the Grave,
The breath from the depths of the Sea,
The breath of Tomorrow:
By the white and dark winds of the world,
The four and the three that are seven,
That Man knoweth,
That One dreadeth,
That God blesseth —

Be all well
On mountain and moorland and lea,
On loch-face and lochan and river,
On shore and shallow and sea!

Windy Nights

ROBERT LOUIS STEVENSON

Whenever the moon and stars are set,
Whenever the wind is high,
All night long in the dark and wet,
A man goes riding by.
Late in the night when the fires are out,
Why does he gallop and gallop about?

Whenever the trees are crying aloud,
And ships are tossed at sea,
By, on the highway, low and loud,
By at the gallop goes he.
By at the gallop he goes, and then
By he comes back at the gallop again.

The Four Brothers

ANONYMOUS

Hithery, hethery — I love best
The wind that blows from out the West,
Breathing balm, and scent of musk,
Rosy at morning, rosy at dusk.

Wind from the North, Oho and Oho!
Climbs with his white mules laden with snow;
Up through the mirk plod, muffled by,
Master and mules through the labouring sky.

Wind from the South lags back again
With bags of jewels from out of Spain;
A hole in the corner, and out they come —
May-bud, apple-bud, bramble-bloom.

Black runs the East, with clouded hair,
Grim as a spectre through the air,
And with his lash, drives in again
Beasts to stall — to their fireside men.

From *Ode to the West Wind*

PERCY BYSSHE SHELLEY

... Be thou, Spirit fierce,
My spirit! Be thou me, impetuous one!

Drive my dead thoughts over the universe
Like withered leaves to quicken a new birth!
And, by the incantation of this verse,

Scatter, as from an unextinguished hearth
Ashes and sparks, my words among mankind!
Be through my lips to unawakened earth

The trumpet of a prophecy! O, Wind,
If Winter comes, can Spring be far behind?

The Mischievous Wind

CHRISTINA T. OWEN

The wind is such a playful chap;
Today he snatched my new spring hat.
He tossed it in the air so high
I saw it sailing through the sky.
I knew I'd never get it back —
Then, down he dropped it in my lap!

The Wind

ANONYMOUS

When the wind is in the east
'Tis good for neither man nor beast
When the wind is in the north,
The skilful fisher goes not forth;
When the wind is in the south,
It blows the bait in the fishes' mouth;
When the wind is in the west,
Then 'tis at the very best.

Windy Nights

RODNEY BENNETT

Rumbling in the chimneys,
Ratttling at the doors,
Round the roofs and round the roads
The rude wind roars;
Raging through the darkness,
Raving through the trees,
Racing off again across
The great grey seas.

Ode to the North-East Wind

CHARLES KINGSLEY

Welcome, wild North-easter!
  Shame it is to see
Odes to every zephyr;
  Ne'er a verse to thee.
Welcome, black North-easter!
  O'er the German foam;
O'er the Danish moorlands,
  From thy frozen home.
Tired are we of summer,
  Tired of gaudy glare,
Showers soft and steaming,
  Hot and breathless air.
Tired of listless dreaming,
  Through the lazy day:
Jovial wind of winter,
  Turn us out to play!
Sweep the golden reed-beds;
  Crisp the lazy dyke;
Hunger into madness
  Every plunging pike.
Fill the lake with wild-fowl;
  Fill the marsh with snipe;
While on dreary moorlands
  Lonely curlew pipe.
Through the black fir-forest
  Thunder harsh and dry,
Shattering down the snowflakes
  Off the curdled sky.
Hark! The brave North-easter!
  Breast-high lies the scent,
On by holt and headland,
  Over heath and bent.
Chime, ye dappled starlings
  Through the sleet and snow
Who can over-ride you?
  Let the horses go!

Chime, ye dappled darlings,
    Down the roaring blast;
You shall see a fox die
    Ere an hour be past.
Go! and rest tomorrow,
    Hunting in your dreams,
While our skates are ringing
    O'er the frozen streams.
Let the luscious South-wind
    Breathe in lovers' sighs,
While the lazy gallants
    Bask in ladies' eyes.
What does he but soften
    Heart alike and pen?
'Tis the hard grey weather
    Breeds hard English men.
What's the soft South-wester?
    'Tis the ladies' breeze,
Bringing home their true-loves
    Out of all the seas:
But the black North-easter,
    Through the snowstorm hurled,
Drives our English hearts of oak
    Seaward around the world.
Come, as came our fathers,
    Heralded by thee,
Conquering from the eastward,
    Lords by land and sea.
Come; and strong within us
    Stir the Viking's blood;
Bracing brain and sinew;
    Blow, thou wind of God!

Wasser und Feuer

FRIEDRICH SCHILLER

Und es wallet und woget und brauset und zischt
Wie wenn Wasser mit Feuer sich menget und mischt.

Fire

FRIEDRICH NIETZSCHE

Yea, my origin I know
Hungry as the fire's glow,
Burning and consuming me,
Light it is to which I cleave,
Carbon only which I leave,
Fire am I, certainly.

Fire

MARGARET MORGAN

Fire am I!
With crackling, roaring flame I come,
Can ye not hear me?

Fire am I!
With brilliant, blinding flame I come,
Can ye not see me?

Fire am I!
With searing, scorching flame I come,
Can ye not feel me?

Fire am I!
With all the power of flame I come,
Can ye not quench me?

Fire am I!
With leaping tongues of flame I come,
Are ye not consumed by me?

Fire am I!
With pure enlightening flame I come,
Are ye not inspired by me?

Fire am I!
Are ye not changed by me?

Light — all creating

MARGARET MORGAN

Into the world it streams —
    Illuminating;

Directness it pursues —
    Vindicating;

From captivity it escapes —
    Liberating;

Illusion it loves to weave —
    Intoxicating;

Life and warmth it bears —
    Generating;

Into being it bursts —
    Irradiating;

Light — all creating.

Desert

TREVOR SMITH WESTGARTH

Sand is to desert as water is to sea,
It rises, falls and onward goes
As far as the eye can see.
And the sun looks down like a staring eye
With fierce and angry glare,
All hotness in its temper,
From dawn to dusk beware,
For if a hot wind rises
It lifts the silken sand
And throws into face and eye
Like a cruel and bitter hand.
No grass or tree is seen there,
No sound from bird or beast,
But only sand and heat and sand
To the North, South, West and East.

The Gnome

MARGARET MORGAN

Deep down he goes, the little gnome,
Deep down into his earthy home.
Deep down among the roots he lives;
Such help to all the plants he gives.

He helps the seed to split its skin;
He helps the roots to settle in;
He helps the shoots to stand upright
And grow to reach the warm sunlight.

Sometimes he comes above the ground;
Sometimes his footprints can be found;
Sometimes, before the moon is up,
He drinks the dew from bluebell cups.

I Knew a Gnome

TREVOR SMITH WESTGARTH

I knew a gnome
Who had his home
Right in the middle of an oak tree.
He wore a hat
And breeches that
Were all of the colour of the oak tree.
Two squirrels lived above his head,
Some rabbits burrowed beneath his bed,
"I keep them warm and safe," he said,
"All in the middle of my oak tree."

A wise old owl
She found a hole
High in the trunk of the oak tree.
And come what may
She slept all day
High in the trunk of the oak tree.

But when at last she took her flight,
Hooting in the pale moonlight,
The gnome rode on her back all night,
Swooping all around about his oak tree.

Overheard on a Saltmarsh

HAROLD MONRO

Nymph, nymph, what are your beads?
Green glass, goblin. Why do you stare at them?
Give them me.
  No.
Give them me. Give them me.
  No.
Then I will howl all night in the reeds,
Lie in the mud and howl for them.

Goblin, why do you love them so?

They are better than stars or water,
Better than voices of winds that sing,
Better than any man's fair daughter,
Your green glass beads on a silver ring.

Hush I stole them out of the moon.

Give me your beads, I want them.
  No.
I will howl in a deep lagoon
For your green glass beads, I love them so.
Give them me. Give them.
  No.

Far Over the Misty Mountains

J.R.R. TOLKIEN

Far over the misty mountains cold
To dungeons deep and caverns old
We must away ere break of day
To seek the pale enchanted gold.

The dwarves of yore made mighty spells,
While hammers fell like ringing bells
In places deep, where dark things sleep,
In hollow halls beneath the fells.

For ancient king and elvish lord
There many a gleaming golden hoard
They shaped and wrought, and light they caught
To hide in gems on hilt of sword.

On silver necklaces they strung
The flowering stars, on crowns they hung
The dragon-fire, in twisted wire
They meshed the light of moon and sun.

Far over the misty mountains cold
To dungeons deep and caverns old
We must away, ere break of day,
To claim our long-forgotten gold.

Goblets they carved there for themselves
And harps of gold; where no man delves
There lay they long, and many a song
Was sung unheard by men or elves.

The pines were roaring on the height,
The winds were moaning in the night,
The fire was red, it flaming spread;
The trees like torches blazed with light.

The bells were ringing in the dale
And men looked up with faces pale;
The dragon's ire more fierce than fire
Laid low their towers and houses frail.

The mountains smoked beneath the moon;
The dwarves, they heard the tramp of doom.
They fled their hall to dying fall
Beneath his feet, beneath the moon.

Far over the misty mountains grim
To dungeons deep and caverns dim
We must away, ere break of day,
To win our harps and gold from him!

The Ancient Elf

JAMES STEPHENS

I am the maker,
The builder, the breaker,
The eagle-winged helper,
The speedy forsaker!

The lance and the lyre,
The water, the fire,
The tooth of oppression,
The lip of desire!

The snare and the wing,
The honey, the sting!
When you seek for me — look
For a different thing.

I, careless and gay,
Never mean what I say,
For my thoughts and my eyes
Look the opposite way!

The Temptation of St Anthony

FRENCH

Goblins came on mischief bent
To Saint Anthony in Lent.

Come ye goblins small and big,
We will kill the hermit's pig.

While the good monk minds his book,
We the hams will cure and cook.

While he goes down on his knees,
We will fry the sausages.

On his knees went Anthony
To those imps of Barbary.

Good kind goblins, spare his life,
He to me is child and wife.

He is my felicity,
Spare, O spare my pig to me.

But the pig they did not spare,
Did not heed the hermit's prayer.

While the good monk read his book,
They the hams did cure and cook.

Still he rose not from his knees,
While they fried the sausages.

All at once the morning broke,
From his dreams the monk awoke.

There in the kind light of day
Was the little pig at play.

– – – ❖ – – –

Flowers and Trees

– – – ❖ – – –

From *Flower Fairies of the Autumn*

CICELY MARY BARKER

The Song of the Acorn Fairy

To English folk the mighty oak
    Is England's noblest tree;
Its hard-grained wood is strong and good
    As English hearts can be.
And would you know how oak trees grow,
    The secret may be told:
You do but need to plant for seed
    One acorn in the mould;
For even so, long years ago,
    Were born the oaks of old.

The Song of the Blackberry Fairy

My berries cluster black and thick
For rich and poor alike to pick.
I'll tear your dress, and cling, and tease
And scratch your hands and arms and knees.
I'll stain your fingers and your face,
And then I'll laugh at your disgrace.
But when the bramble-jelly's made,
You'll find your trouble well repaid.

The Song of the Crab-apple Fairy

Crab-apples, crab-apples, out in the wood,
Little and bitter, yet little and good!

>>

The apples in orchards, so rosy and fine,
Are children of wild little apples like mine.

The branches are laden, and droop to the ground;
The fairy-fruit falls in a circle around;
Now all you good children, come gather them up:
They'll make you sweet jelly to spread when you sup.

One little apple I'll catch for myself;
I'll stew it and strain it, to store on a shelf
In four or five acorn-cups, locked with a key
In a cupboard of mine at the root of the tree.

The Holly Fairy
O, I am green in Winter-time,
When other trees are brown;
Of all the trees (so saith the rhyme)
The holly bears the crown.
December days are drawing near
When I shall come to town,
And carol-boys go singing clear
Of all the trees (O hush and hear!)
The holly bears the crown!
For who so well-beloved and merry
As the scarlet Holly Berry?

The Song of the Bluebell Fairy
My hundred thousand bells of blue,
The splendour of the Spring,
They carpet all the woods anew
With royalty of sapphire hue;
The primrose is the Queen, 'tis true
But surely I am King!
Ah, yes,
The peerless Woodland King!

Loud, loud the thrushes sing their song;
The bluebell woods are wide;
My stems are tall and straight and strong;
From ugly streets the children throng,
They gather armfuls, great and long,

Then home they troop in pride —
Ah, yes,
With laughter and with pride!

Narcissus

Brown bulbs were buried deep;
Now, from the kind old earth,
Out of the winter's sleep,
Comes a new birth!

Flowers on stems that sway;
Flowers of snowy white,
Flowers as sweet as day,
After the night.

So does Narcissus bring
Tidings most glad and plain:
"Winter's gone; here is the Spring —
Easter again!"

Geranium

Red, red, vermillion red,
With buds and blooms in glorious head!
There isn't a flower, the wide world through,
That glows with a brighter scarlet hue.
Her name — Geranium — everyone knows;
She's just as happy wherever she grows,
In an earthen pot or a garden bed
Red, red, vermillion red!

The Song of the Heather Fairy

"Ho, Heather, Ho! From south to north
Spread now your royal purple forth!
Ho, jolly one! From east to west,
The moorland waiteth to be dressed!"

"I come, I come! With footsteps sure
I run to clothe the waiting moor;
From heath to heath I leap and stride
To fling my bounty far and wide."

TRADITIONAL

Lilies are white
Rosemary's green
When you are king
I will be queen.

Roses are red
Lavender's blue
If you will have me
I will have you.

Little White Lily

GEORGE MACDONALD

Little white Lily sat by a stone,
Drooping and waiting till the sun shone.
Little white Lily sunshine has fed;
Little white Lily is lifting her head.

Little white Lily smells very sweet;
On her head sunshine, rain at her feet.
Thanks to the sunshine, thanks to the rain!
Little white Lily is happy again.

The Country Cousin

OLIN WANNAMAKER

Once a country Buttercup
In a city bed woke up.
All the Daisies turned away;
None invited her to stay.

When the gardener came, he said,
While he made the Daisies' bed,
"Wild flower, this is not the place
To show your little sunburnt face."

But he kindly dug her up
O, the trembling Buttercup! —
Bore her in a clod of earth
Where she should have waked at birth;
Set her in a soft, rich place
With other flowers of her race.

The Small Celandine

William Wordsworth

There is a flower, the lesser Celandine,
That shrinks, like many more, from cold and rain;
And, the first moment that the sun may shine,
Bright as the sun himself, 'tis out again!

When hailstones have been falling, swarm on swarm,
Or blasts the green fields and the trees distrest,
Oft have I seen it muffled up from harm
In close self-shelter, like a Thing at rest.

But lately, one rough day, this flower I passed
And recognised it, though an altered form,
Now standing forth an offering to the blast,
And buffeted at will by rain and storm.

I stopped, and said with inly-muttered voice,
"It doth not love the shower, nor seek the cold:
This neither is its courage nor its choice,
But its necessity in being old.

The sunshine may not cheer it, nor the dew;
It cannot help itself in its decay;
Stiff in its members, withered, changed of hue."
And, in my spleen, I smiled that it was grey.

To be a Prodigal's Favourite — then, worse truth,
A Miser's Pensioner — behold our lot!
O Man, that from thy fair and shining youth
Age might but take the things Youth needed not!

Pimpernel

CHARLOTTE DRUITT COLE

I'm the pert little pimpernel,
Who ever so cleverly weather foretells;
If I open my eye,
There's a cloudless sky;
If I shut it again,
Then it's sure to rain.

The Daffodils

WILLIAM WORDSWORTH

I wandered lonely as a cloud
That floats on high o'er vales and hills,
When all at once I saw a crowd,
A host, of golden daffodils;
Beside the lake, beneath the trees,
Fluttering and dancing in the breeze.

Continuous as the stars that shine
And twinkle on the Milky Way,
They stretched in never-ending line
Along the margin of a bay:
Ten thousand saw I at a glance,
Tossing their heads in sprightly dance.

The waves beside them danced; but they
Out-did the sparkling waves in glee:
A poet could not but be gay,
In such a jocund company:
I gazed — and gazed — but little thought
What wealth the show to me had brought:

For oft, when on my couch I lie
In vacant or in pensive mood,
They flash upon that inward eye
Which is the bliss of solitude;
And then my heart with pleasure fills,
And dances with the daffodils.

The Oak and the Reed

MARGARET MORGAN

The great oak tree
Thinks he's the strongest
As he's been standing
There the longest.

The wind it blew,
The rain came lashing;
And down the great oak tree
Came crashing.

The slender reed
She knows much better,
For she can bend
In stormy weather.

The slender reed
Swayed in the weather,
And at the dawn
Was strong as ever.

The Coming Storm

MATTHEW BROWNE

The treetops rustle, the treetops wave,
They hustle, they bustle, and down in a cave
The winds are murmuring ready to rave.
The skies are dimming, the birds fly low,
Skimming and swimming, their wings are slow,
The dead leaves hurry, the waters too
Flurry and scurry as if they knew
A storm was at hand, the smoke is blue.

Loveliest of Trees

A.E. HOUSMAN

Loveliest of trees, the cherry now
Is hung with bloom along the bough,
And stands about the woodland ride
Wearing white for Eastertide.

Now, of my three score years and ten,
Twenty will not come again,
And take from seventy springs a score,
It leaves me only fifty more.

And since to look at things in bloom
Fifty springs are little room,
About the woodlands I will go
To see the cherry hung with snow.

Poplars

ANONYMOUS

Seven lovely poplars
Swaying in the breeze.
Seven softly sighing
Tall and slender trees.

Silvered by the moonlight
Pointing to the sky:
Look, like leafy spears, they
Hold the stars on high.

Trees

SARA COLERIDGE

The Oak is called the King of Trees,
The Aspen quivers in the breeze,
The Poplar grows up straight and tall,
The Pear tree spreads along the wall,
The Sycamore gives pleasant shade,
The Willow droops in watery glade,
The Fir tree useful timber gives,
The Beech amid the forest lives.

Trees

WALTER DE LA MARE

Of all the trees in England,
    Her sweet three corners in,
Only the Ash, the bonnie Ash
    Burns fierce while it is green.

Of all the trees in England,
    From sea to sea again,
The Willow loveliest stoops her boughs
    Beneath the driving rain.

Of all the trees in England,
    Past frankincense and myrrh,
There's none for smell, of bloom and smoke,
    Like Lime and Juniper.

Of all the trees in England,
    Oak, Elder, Elm and Thorn,
The Yew alone burns lamps of peace
    For them that lie forlorn.

Log fires

ANONYMOUS

Beechwood fires are bright and clear,
If the logs are kept a year;
Chestnut only good, they say,
If for long it's laid away;
Make a fire of *Elder* tree,
Death within your house shall be;
But *Ash* new or *Ash* old
Is fit for Queen with crown of gold.

Birch and *Fir* logs burn too fast,
Blaze up bright and do not last;
It is by the Irish said
Hawthorn bakes the sweetest bread;
Elmwood burns like churchyard mould —
E'en the very flames are cold;
But *Ash* green or *Ash* brown
Is fit for Queen with golden crown.

Poplar gives a bitter smoke,
Fills your eyes and makes you choke;
Apple wood will scent your room
With an incense-like perfume.
Oaken logs, if dry and old,
Keep away the winter's cold;
But *Ash* wet or *Ash* dry
A King shall warm his slippers by.

Logs to Burn

OLD SUSSEX POEM

Logs to burn, logs to burn,
Logs to save the coal a turn.
Here's a word to make you wise
When you hear the woodman's cries.

Never heed his usual tale
That he has good logs for sale,
But read these lines and really learn
The proper kinds of logs to burn.

Oaken logs will warm you well
If they're old and dry.
Larch logs of pinewood smell
But the sparks will fly.

Beech logs for Christmas time,
Yew logs they heat well.
"Scotch" logs it is a crime
For anyone to sell.

Birch logs will burn too fast,
Chestnut scarce at all,
Hawthorn logs are good to last
If cut in the fall.

Cherry logs across the days
Smell like flowers in bloom.
But ash logs, all smooth and grey —
Burn them green or old;
Buy up all that come your way,
They're worth their weight in gold.

Earth, Sun and Stars

Precious Stones

CHRISTINA ROSSETTI

An emerald is as green as grass,
A ruby red as blood,
A sapphire shines as blue as heaven,
But a flint lies in the mud.

A diamond is a brilliant stone
To catch the world's desire,
An opal holds a rainbow light,
But a flint holds fire.

Planets and Metals

From *The Young Scientist's Companion*

MAURICE GOLDSMITH

Like the planets up in heaven,
Metals also number seven;
Copper, iron, silver, gold,
Tin and lead, to smelt and mould
Cosmos gave us; listen further:
Fiery sulphur was their father,
And their mother — mercury,
That, my son, is known to me.

Poem to the Sun

IRENE GOODMAN

Great, pure and shining orb,
Celestial in thy might
Let lowly earth absorb
Thy wondrous healing light.

Feeling thy mighty ray,
Descending from on high,
Summon all life thy way,
Ascending to the sky.

Pour out thy bounteous balm
On man and beast and tree
That each may by thy charm
A purer being be.

Hymn to the Sun

ALFRED, LORD TENNYSON

Once again thou flamest heavenward
Once again we see thee rise
Every morning is thy birthday
Gladdening human hearts and eyes.

Every morning here we greet thee
Bowing lowly down before thee —
Thee the Godlike, Thee the changeless,
In thine ever-changing skies.

From *The Sun*

CHRISTIAN MORGENSTERN

"I am the sun, and I bear with my might
The earth by day and the earth by night.
I hold her fast and my gifts I bestow
That everything on her may live and grow ..."

O Lady Moon

CHRISTINA ROSSETTI

O Lady Moon, your horns point to the East;
  Shine, be increased!
O Lady Moon, your horns point to the West;
  Wane, be at rest!

The Moon

PERCY BYSSHE SHELLEY

That orbid maiden, with white fire laden,
Whom mortals call the Moon,
Glides glimmering o'er my fleece-like floor,
By the midnight breezes strewn.

Sun and Moon

God with all-commanding might
Filled the new-made world with light.
He the golden-tressed sun
All day caused his course to run,
And the moon to shine by night
With her spangled sisters bright.

FRANCIS THOMPSON

All things by immortal power
Near or far
Hiddenly
To each other linked are,
That thou canst not stir a flower
Without troubling of a star.

Hymn to the North Star

WILLIAM CULLEN BRYANT

Constellations come, and climb the heavens, and go,
And thou dost see them rise,
Star of the Pole! and thou dost see them set.
Alone in thy cold skies,
Thou keep'st thine old unmoving station yet
Nor join'st the dances of that glittering train,
Nor dipp'st thy virgin orb in the blue western main.

On thy unaltering blaze
The half-wrecked mariner, his compass lost,
Fixes his steadfast gaze,
And steers, undoubting, to the friendly coast;
And those who stray in perilous wastes by night
Are glad when thou dost shine to guide their footsteps right.

My Father's House

ANONYMOUS

Transfixed at Heaven's Gate I stand
And quite forget this twilight land.
For oh, my Father's House doth shine
With streams of beauty crystalline!
The doors of heaven stand ajar,
Each portal opens on a star;
Into my Father's House I gaze
And see His Palace all ablaze:
With fiery torches, quenchless, white,
With ageless grandeur, beauty bright.

The Lost Star

FIONA MACLEOD

A star was loosed from heaven;
All saw it fall, in wonder,
Where universe clashed universe
With solar thunder.

The angels praised God's glory,
To send this beacon-flare
To show the terror of darkness
Beneath the Golden Stair.

But God was brooding only
Upon new births of light;
The star was a drop of water
On the lips of Eternal Light.

Nightfall

PETER BATESON

When sleeping I lie, and dark night falls,
An angel draws nigh and softly calls
And touches my eyes, my mouth, my hands,
And leads me over rainbow strands
To shining halls in a starry land.

The fairest children of the sun,
The sister of the moon at play,
The smiling stars around me run
And kiss my brow and bid me stay.

They sing to me sweetly all the night
And show me their pictures of living light,
And when I return and morning is come
Their voices echo on and on,
The heavenly children of the sun.

From *The Pythagorean Liturgy*

Though in noon's heaven no star you see,
Know well that many there must be.
And with your soul's extended ears
You'll hear the music of the spheres.

Day and Night

FIONA MACLEOD

From grey of dusk, the veils unfold
To pearl and amethyst and gold —
    Thus is the new day woven and spun:

From glory of blue to rainbow-spray,
From sunset-gold to violet-grey —
    Thus is the restful night re-won.

From *An Essay on Man*

ALEXANDER POPE

He, who through vast immensity can pierce,
Sees worlds on worlds compose one universe,
Observe how system into system runs,
What other planets circle other suns,
What varied being peoples every star,
May tell why Heaven has made us as we are.

Vision of the Universe

GIORDANO BRUNO

I cleave the sky, and other suns behold.
Celestial worlds innumerable I see:
One goes, another company appears.
My opinion fails not, and my heart is bold
To journey on through all.

The Eternal Mind

FROM JANUARY NIGHT SKY, *DAILY TELEGRAPH,* 1983

Beneath this world of stars and flowers
That rolls in visible deity,
I dream another world is ours
And is the soul of all we see.
It hath no form, it hath no spirit;
It is perchance the Eternal mind;
Beyond the sense that we inherit
I feel it dim and undefined.

Light

F.W. BOURDILLON

The night has a thousand eyes,
    And the day but one;
Yet the light of the bright world dies
    With the dying sun.

The mind has a thousand eyes,
    And the heart but one;
Yet the light of a whole life dies
    When love is done.

A Limerick

There was a young lady called Bright
Who could travel much faster than light.
    She set off one day
    In a relative way
And came back the previous night.

Divine Geometry

From *Dante's Divine Comedy Paradiso*

TRANSLATED BY DOROTHY L. SAYERS

As the geometer his mind applies
To square the circle, not for all his wit
Finds the right formula, howe'er he tries,

So strove I with wonder — how to fit
The image of the sphere; so sought to see
How it maintained the point of rest in it.

Thither my own wings could not carry me,
But that a flash my understanding clove,
Whence its desire came to it suddenly.

High phantasy lost power and here broke off;
Yet as a wheel moves smoothly, free from jars
My will and my desire were turned by love,

The love that moves the sun and the other stars.

— — — ❖ — — —

Seasons

— — — ❖ — — —

The Crowning of the Year

JULIET COMPTON-BURNETT

The months weave a garland to crown the year,
Its jewels are the leaves and the flowers
The golden sun and the twinkling stars
The wind and the snow and the showers.
Colour and beauty from far and near
Weaving a garland to crown the year.

January brings the snow
But hark, the roots begin to grow.

February brings flowers of light
Petals three of snowdrops white.

March's blossoms — purple, gold,
Six petals to the sun unfold.

April's here, gold trumpets sound
And stars of white bedeck the ground.

May is the month of pink and white
Apple, May, and Parsley light.

June brings flowers of rainbow hue
Crimson, gold, and heavenly blue.

Flowers gay we still may see
Though dark the green on *July's* tree.

Yellow turn the fields of grain
In *August* sun and *August* rain.

September's fruits grow good to see
On pear and plum and apple tree.

October's leaves come fluttering down
In shades of red and gold and brown.

November's gift is rich and rare
The beauty of the branches bare.

December's joy in each heart glows
For then was born the Christmas rose.

Colour and beauty from far and near
Weaving a garland to crown the year.

Seasons

DAVID KUHRT

The few remaining summer leaves shrivel
and death's lace, hung for the saints of summer fire falls.
The first sharp breath of winter cuts the thread
and dust, fingered finely by the sun, drops down
where earth's aspiring substance filtered through the stems in spring.

Gathered at the extremities of green twigs
the body of last year's fallen sun is raised incorruptible,
and our cold faces, cracked with pent-up mirth, laugh
as the dirge of north winds dies, and gothic trees,
urged to exultations of green leaves, unfold their winter meditations.

Summer and Winter

RUDOLF STEINER
Translated by George and Mary Adams

Asleep is the soul of Earth
In Summer's heat,
While the Sun's outward Glory
Rays through the realms of Space.

Awake is the soul of Earth
In Winter's cold,
While the Sun's inmost Being
Lightens in Spirit.

Summer's day of joy
For Earth is sleep.
Winter's holy night
For Earth is day.

Seasons and Archangels

ISABEL WYATT

Thou Gabriel!
Bring me the white stars of winter,
    Of thy lilies and snows;
Till the blessing of life-giving water and moon-beam
    Into me flows.

Thou Raphael!
Bring me the green grace of springtime
    Of blithe sap and young leaves;
Till the blessing of breathing and music and healing
    Into me weaves.

Thou Uriel!
Bring me the red flame of summer
From air's golden steeps;
Till the blessing of fires of the rose and the rainbow
Into me leaps.

Thou Michael!
Plunge deep the blue sword of autumn
Where the dark dragon lurks;
Till the stirring of iron in the blood and the meteor
Into me works.

Calendar Months

TRADITIONAL

Thirty days hath September,
April, June, and November.
All the rest have thirty-one
Excepting February alone
Which has twenty-eight days clear
And twenty-nine in each leap year.

Calendar Rhyme

FLORA WILLIS WATSON

In January falls the snow,
In February cold winds blow,
In March peep out the early flowers,
And April comes with sunny showers.
In May the roses bloom so gay,
In June the farmer mows his hay,
In July brightly shines the sun,
In August harvest is begun.
September turns the green leaves brown,
October winds then shake them down,
November fills with bleak and drear,
December comes and ends the year.

Autumn

Michael the Victorious

FROM THE *CARMINA GADELICA*

Thou Michael the Victorious!
I make my circuit under thy shield.
Thou Michael of the white steed
And of the bright, brilliant blade!
Conqueror of the dragon
Be thou at my back.
Thou ranger of the heavens!
Thou warrior of the King of all!
    O Michael the Victorious
    My pride and my guide!
    O Michael the Victorious
    The glory of mine eye.

I make my circuit
In the fellowship of my saint,
On the machair, on the meadow,
On the cold heathery hill;
Though I should travel ocean
And the hard globe of the world,
No harm can e'er befall me
'Neath the shelter of thy shield;
    O Michael the Victorious,
    Jewel of my heart,
    O Michael the Victorious,
    God's shepherd thou art.

Be the sacred Three of Glory
Aye at peace with me,
With my horses, with my cattle,
With my woolly sheep in flocks.
With the crops growing in the field
Or ripening in the sheaf,

On the machair, on the moor,
In cole, in heap, or stack.
    Every thing on high or low,
    Every furnishing and flock,
    Belong to the holy Triune of Glory
    And to Michael the Victorious.

St Michael's Harvest Song

ANONYMOUS

In autumn Saint Michael with sword and with shield
Passes over meadow and orchard and field.
He's on the path to battle 'gainst darkness and strife —
He is the heavenly warrior protector of life.

The harvest let us gather with Michael's aid;
The light he sheddeth fails not nor does it fade,
And when the corn is cut and the meadows are bare
We'll don Saint Michael's armour and onward we'll fare.

We are Saint Michael's warriors with strong heart and mind,
We forge our way through darkness Saint Michael to find.
And there he stands in glory; Saint Michael we pray,
Lead us into battle and show us thy way.

Autumn

TRADITIONAL

Yellow the bracken,
    Golden the sheaves,
Rosy the apples,
    Crimson the leaves;
Mist on the hillside,
    Clouds grey and white.
Autumn, good morning!
    Summer, good night!

I Will Go with my Father a-Ploughing

SEOSMH MACCATHMHAOIL

I will go with my father a-ploughing,
To the green field by the sea,
And the rooks and the crows and the seagulls
Will come flocking after me.
I will sing to the patient horses
With the lark in the white of the air,
And my father will sing the plough song
That blesses the cleaving share.

I will go with my father a-sowing
To the red field by the sea,
And the rooks and the gulls and the starlings
Will come flocking after me.
I will sing to the striding sowers
With the finch on the flowering sloe,
And my father will sing the seed song
That only the wise men know.

I will go with my father a-reaping
To the brown field by the sea,
And the geese and the crows and the children
Will come flocking after me.
I will sing to the weary reapers
With the wren in the heat of the sun,
And my father will sing the scythe song
That joys for the harvest done.

TRADITIONAL

We've ploughed our fields
We've sown our seed
We've made all neat and gay.
    Then take a bit, and leave a bit
    Away, birds, away!

The Wind and the Leaves

TRADITIONAL

Come, little leaves, said the wind one day,
Come over the meadows with me and play.
Put on your dresses of red and gold,
For summer is gone and the days grow cold.

Soon as the leaves heard the wind's loud call
Down they came fluttering, one and all.
Over the fields they danced and flew,
Singing the soft little songs they knew.

Dancing and whirling the little leaves went,
Winter had called them, and they were content
Soon fast asleep on their earthly beds,
The snow laid a coverlet on their heads.

Red in Autumn

ELIZABETH GOULD

Tipperty-Toes, the smallest elf,
Sat on a mushroom by himself.
Playing a little tinkling tune
Under the big round harvest moon;
And this is the song that Tipperty made
To sing to the little tune he played.

"Red are the hips, red are the haws,
Red and gold are the leaves that fall,
Red are the poppies in the corn,
Red berries on the rowan tall;
Red is the big round harvest moon,
And red are my new little dancing shoon."

Little red leaves are glad today
For the wind is blowing them off and away.
They're flying here, they're flying there,
Little red leaves, you're everywhere!

Class One Song

TREVOR SMITH WESTGARTH

The rabbit twitched his long brown ears
On a lovely September day,
He heard the North wind whistle
And scampered off to say,
"Hurry, hurry, hurry, hurry,
Autumn's on its way!"

The bee was buzzing round some flowers
On a lovely September day,
He saw the roses' petals fall
And he flew off to say,
"Hurry, hurry, hurry, hurry,
Autumn's on its way!"

The squirrel ran along a branch
On a lovely September day,
He found a nut all golden brown
And scurried off to say,
"Hurry, hurry, hurry, hurry,
Autumn's on its way!"

A hedgehog sniffed his little snout
On a lovely September day,
He smelt the leaves all damp and brown
And scampered off to say,
"Hurry, hurry, hurry, hurry,
Autumn's on its way!"

Autumn Poem

EMILY BRONTË

Fall, leaves, fall;
Die, flowers, away;
Lengthen night and shorten day.
Every leaf speaks bliss to me
Fluttering from the Autumn tree
I shall smile when wreaths of snow
Blossom where the rose should grow
I shall sing when night's decay
Ushers in a drearier day.

Alchemy

DAVID KUHRT

The last leaves of autumn fire
have fallen on the forest floor
where dead wood crumbles into dust
and insects bury the fallen sun
golden on the ground.

Cutting the last links with life
high winds gather the leaves,
the last traceable elements of sun,
in pyres to burn, fire and earth,
and constitute in substance gold
to crown the sun king or celebrate rebirth.

Perennially the tanist comes
and the old king's fallen crown is raised,
gold, incorruptible,
transformations of the earth
inauspiciously accomplished.

Harvest

MOLLY DE HAVAS

Fields of wheat and oats and barley
Bending in the summer breeze,
Sun and shadow, wave and ripple,
Chase across their golden seas.

Wheat stands tall and straight and heavy,
Oat grains hang in separate drops,
Barley's whiskered head curves over —
Gold, and brown, and yellow crops.

When the corn is fully ripened
Then the harvest is begun.
Reaping, binding, on the stubble
Stacking sheaves beneath the sun.

Now we load the great farm wagons
Working till the field is clear.
Stubble soon must turn to ploughland
Ready for another year.

October

TRADITIONAL

Golden is the garden,
Golden is the glen,
Golden, golden, golden,
October's here again.

Golden are the tree-tops,
Golden is the sky,
Golden, golden, golden,
October's here again.

The Poem of Hallowe'en Lanterns

ANONYMOUS

Beautiful are forests when the leaves are green;
Beautiful are rainbows where a storm has been;
Beautiful are lanterns in the night at Hallowe'en.

Beautiful are lanterns gilding spring's gay shoots;
Beautiful are lanterns firing autumn's fruits;
Beautiful are lanterns carved from winter's earthy roots.

Poem for Hallowe'en

Hallowe'en lanterns swinging soft and slow,
Hallowe'en lanterns filled with candle glow
Gently shining candles, cupped in caves of rosy snow.

Vegetable faces in a flickering fire
Shimmer on the darkness sway and pause awhile,
On each brow a brightness and a star behind each smile.

Hallowe'en

LEONARD CLARK

This is the night when witches fly
On their whizzing broomsticks through the wintry sky;
Steering up the pathway where the stars are strewn,
They stretch skinny fingers to the waking moon.

This is the night when angels go
In and out the houses, winging o'er the snow;
Clearing out the demons from the countryside,
They make it new and ready for Christmastide.

The Hag

ROBERT HERRICK

The Hag is astride,
This night for to ride;
The Devil and she together:
Through thick and through thin,
Now out and then in,
Though ne'er so foul be the weather.

A thorn or a burr
She takes for a spur,
With a lash of a bramble she rides now,
Through brakes and through briars
O'er ditches and mires,
She follows the spirit that guides now.

No Beast for his food
Dares now range the wood,
But hushed in his lair he lies lurking,
While mischiefs, by these,
On land and on seas,
At noon of night are awaking.

The storm will arise
And trouble the skies;
This night and more for the wonder,
The ghost from the tomb
Affrighted shall come,
Called out by the clap of the thunder.

Please to Remember

WALTER DE LA MARE

Here am I,
A poor old Guy:
Legs in a bonfire,
Head in the sky;

Shoeless my toes,
Wild stars behind,
Smoke in my nose,
And my eye-peeps blind;

Old hat, old straw —
In this disgrace;
While the wildfire gleams
On a mask for face.

Ay, all I am made of
Only trash is;
And soon — soon,
Will be dust and ashes.

November

HARTLEY COLERIDGE

The mellow year is hastening to its close;
The little birds have almost sung their last,
Their small notes twitter in the dreary blast —
That shrill-piped harbinger of early snows;
The patient beauty of the scentless rose,
Oft with the morn's hoar crystal quaintly glassed,
Hangs, a pale mourner for the summer past,
And makes a little summer where it grows:
In the chill sunbeam of the faint brief day
The dusky waters shudder as they shine,
The russet leaves obstruct the straggling way
Of oozy brooks, which no deep banks define,
And the gaunt woods, in ragged, scant array,
Wrap their old limbs with sombre ivy twine.

November

MARGARET MORGAN

Now it is November,
Trees are nearly bare;
Red and gold and brown leaves
Scatter everywhere.

Dark now, are the mornings,
Cold and frosty too;
Damp and misty evenings
Chill us through and through.

Busy are all creatures,
Winter food to hide;
Nests to make all cosy,
Warm and safe inside.

November

ANONYMOUS

The loud winds are calling,
The ripe nuts are falling,
The squirrel now gathers his store.
The bears homeward creeping
Will soon all be sleeping
So snugly till winter is o'er.

Winter and Christmas

Winter

MARGARET MORGAN

Blow, North Wind, blow,
All the leaves are falling;
Cold, frost and snow
Winter comes a-calling.
Mother Nature sleeps now,
All the earth is bare;
Deep in the ground
She guards her treasures rare.

Advent

ANONYMOUS

The gift of light
I thankfully hold
And pass to my neighbour
Its shining gold
That everyone may
Feel its glow,
Receiving and giving
May love and grow.

When all our brothers
Have lit their light
No more shall continue
The darkness of night:
But joyful all men
The message shall hear:
"The Christ draws near!"

Advent

ANN ELLERTON

Now the twilight of the year
Comes, and Christmas draweth near.
See, across the Advent sky
How the clouds move quietly.
Earth is waiting, wrapt in sleep,
Waiting in a silence deep.
Birds are hid in bush and reed
Flowers are sleeping in their seed.

Through the woodland to and fro
Silent-footed creatures go.
Hedgehog curled in prickly ball
Burrows 'neath the leaves that fall.
Man and beast and bird and flower
Waiting for the midnight hour
Waiting for the Christ-child's birth
Christ who made the heaven and earth.

Advent

ANONYMOUS

Sun, sun, shining one,
    Have you a gift for my little son?
Moon, moon, glittering one,
    Have you a gift for my little son?
Stars, stars, twinkling ones, ...
Fir tree, fir tree, strong one, ...
Flowers, flowers, fragrant ones, ...
Lamb, lamb, gentle one, ...
Oh children, children of the earth
    Have you a gift for my dear son's birth?

Christmas Night

B.T. Milne

Softly, softly through the darkness
    Snow is falling.
Sharply, sharply in the meadows
    Lambs are calling.
Coldly, coldly all around me
    Winds are blowing.
Brightly, brightly up above me
    Stars are glowing.

Es ist ein Ros' entsprungen

Translated by Eileen Hutchins

There is a rose that blossomed
From out a tender root;
As olden prophets tell us
From Jesse sprang the shoot,
It bore a flower so bright,
Within the bitter winter
On this most holy night.

The rose Isaiah promised,
That bore a bloom on earth,
Was God's own Son eternal,
Whom Mary brought to birth.
In coldest winter's night
She bore her precious burden,
The fairest flower of light.

Carol

WILLIAM CANTON

When the herds were watching
In the midnight chill
Came a spotless lambkin
From the heavenly hill.

Snow was on the mountain
And the wind was cold
When from God's own garden
Dropped a rose of gold.

When 'twas bitter winter,
Houseless and forlorn
In a starlit stable
Christ the Babe was born.

Welcome heavenly lambkin
Welcome, golden rose
Alleluia baby
In the swaddling clothes.

Christmas Night

AFTER KARL SCHUBERT

Over stars is Mary wandering;
In her mantle's flowing folds,
Radiant threads of starlight woven
For her little child she holds.
Throngs of stars behold her passing,
All the sky is filled with light,
With her hands she weaves and gathers
Blessings for the Christmas night.

The Little Fir Tree

MARGARET ROSE

At Christmas time so long ago,
The winds were blowing high and low;
A little green fir tree grew by the Inn,
A little green fir tree straight and slim.
    "Noel, Noel!" the angels sang,
    "Noel, Noel! Goodwill to man."

And, looking up, across the night
The fir tree saw the Star so bright.
The little fir tree wondered why
The star was moving in the sky.
    "Noel, Noel!" ...

The star shone over Bethlehem
Over the stable inn, and then
The little green fir tree shone with light,
Lit by the star that wintry night.
    "Noel, Noel!" ...

The fir tree shone so long ago;
And still in winter's frost and snow,
The little green fir tree comes each year
To bring us joy and Christmas cheer.
    "Noel, Noel!" ...

Carol

TRADITIONAL

I sing of a maiden
That is makè-less;
King of all kings
To her son she ches.

He came all so still
Where his mother was,
As dew in April
That falleth on the grass.

He came all so still
To his mother's bower,
As dew in April
That falleth on the flower.

He came all so still
Where his mother lay,
As dew in April
That falleth on the spray.

Mother and maiden
Was never done but she!
Well may such a lady
Goddess mother be.

Christmas Poem

TRADITIONAL

Above the manger stood a star
A star all wondrous white
And all about His lowly bed
There welled a flood of light.

It bathed the stable in its glow
It shone round Mary's head
And on the kneeling shepherds' cloaks
Its radiant beams were shed.

Star of the world, through time and space
It flames in glory bright
To make man's pilgrimage through the years
A pathway of light.

From *On the Morning of Christ's Nativity*

JOHN MILTON

This is the month, and this the happy morn,
Wherein the Son of heav'n's eternal King,
Of wedded Maid and Virgin Mother born,
Our great redemption from above did bring;
For so the holy sages once did sing,
That he our deadly forfeit should release,
And with his Father work us a perpetual peace.

That glorious form, that light unsufferable,
And that far-beaming blaze of majesty,
Wherewith he wont at heav'n's high council-table
To sit in the midst of Trinal Unity,
He laid aside; and here with us to be,
Forsook the courts of everlasting day,
And chose with us a darksome house of mortal clay.

Say, Heavenly Muse, shall not thy sacred vein
Afford a present to the infant God?
Hast thou no verse, no hymn, or solemn strain,
To welcome him to this his new abode,
Now while the heav'n, by the sun's team untrod,
Hath took no print of the approaching light,
And all the spangled host keep watch in squadrons bright?

See how from far upon the eastern road
The star-led wizards haste with odours sweet!
O run, prevent them with thy humble ode,
And lay it lowly at his blessèd feet;
Have thou the honour first thy Lord to greet,
And join thy voice unto the angel quire,
From out his secret altar touched with hallowed fire ...

Christmas

TRADITIONAL

In my heart a shepherd
In my head a king
Before the Child together
They offer what they bring.

The heart will fire the head
The head will light the heart
The Spirit-Child within
Will know Love's healing art.

In the Heavens a secret
On the earth made known
The Child from Heaven appearing
Love's grace is streaming down.

On the earth is darkness
In the dark shines light
The star proclaims His coming
Illumining the night.

In my heart at midnight
In my head at dark
The angel's song resounding
Kindles afresh Love's spark.

In the world is Christmas,
Christmas lives in me,
Again the Holy Child is born
Love's messenger to be.

Christmas

MARGARET MORGAN

A single Angel came from Heaven
Upon a virgin mild,
And Gabriel to Mary said,
"*You* are to bear God's child."

A single donkey, sure and strong,
With hide of dusty grey,
Nobly carried Mary on
To Beth'lem far away.

A single stable was the only
Shelter they could find,
An ox and ass to share it with
But Mary did not mind.

A single manger was the bed
For Mary's baby boy,
And as she laid Him in the hay
Her heart was filled with joy.

A single shepherd was to see
Bright Angels up above.
He roused his friends, they left their flocks
And sought the King of Love.

A single star shone in the sky
That night so long ago;
Guiding Kings from Eastern lands
Towards the manger low.

A single Baby born on Earth,
God's gift to all mankind
Enters our hearts each Christmastide,
When peace and love we find.

Light of the World

ANN ELLERTON

The Fir tree said,
"I am evergreen,
I remember what has been.
In memory
My candle's light
The Christ-Child's Birth
On Holy Night."

The Chestnut said,
"I look to see
What is now,
What is to be.
My candles flame
When clouds receive Him
In ether spheres
We may perceive Him.
My blossom candle
Flaming tells
Within Earth's aura
Now He dwells."

Light of the World
For Earth He dwells.

The Cradle Song

PADRAIC COLUM

O man from the fields!
Come softly within —
Tread softly, softly,
O man coming in —

Mavourneen is going
From me and from you,
Where Mary will fold him
With mantle of blue —

From reek of the smoke
And cold of the floor
And peering of things
Across the half-door

O man from the fields!
Softly, softly come through
Mary puts round him
Her mantle of blue.

Christmas

REX RAAB

The very heart of heaven
now throbs within the earth,
a secret life is stirring
since heaven's earthly birth.

A secret sound is swelling
that never has been heard,
within the world is working
a clear and sacred word.

The message that it carries
is wrought by God's own art,
the poem of all poems
now moves the human heart.

Christmas Song

E. FIELD

Why do the bells of Christmas ring?
Why do little children sing?
Once a lovely shining star
Seen by shepherds from afar
Gently moved until its light
Made a manger's cradle bright.

There a little baby lay
Pillowed soft upon the hay
And its mother sang and smiled
This is Christ, the holy child.

Therefore bells of Christmas ring,
Therefore little children sing.

The Christmas Rose

ANN ELLERTON

A sign from heaven within the garden grows,
One bloom as if 'twere fashioned all of light,
Blossoming in the depth of Winter's night,
The crown of all the flowers — the Christmas Rose.

Ethereal each lucent petal glows;
Such purity and fragrance seemeth right
Thus to be born when all the world is white,
With Mother Earth wrapt in her mantling snows.
Now at such time, the holiest of the year,
Men of goodwill do celebrate the Birth
Of that most wondrous Rose the Ancients sung.
Now through that hallow'd Child doth Christ appear
Within the troubled stricken realms of Earth,
And from His presence healing Life hath sprung.

Earth's Nuptials

ANN ELLERTON

Twelve days and thirteen nights in all the year
Most holy! Earth is shrouded in a sleep;
Trees sentinel above her, vigil keep.

Their fallen leaves gold tinted once, now sere
With times decaying, wrap her round a'near
To shield her in a covering warm and deep.

And living things within the woodland creep
All silently, that none may see or hear,

Yet though the very breath of life may seem
Suspended in the days and nights of dream —

High festival adorns this hallowed tide,
The starry sphere bends to embrace the Bride,
So greet we now the Harbinger of Birth,
The cosmic marriage of the Heavens and Earth.

Three Kings

ALBERT STEFFEN
Translated by Pauline Wehrle

Three kings, as helpers called, are at your side,
Who point the upward path to worlds so wide,
And guide you inward to the depths of soul.
Yet know that though still distant were the goal,
The earth itself is slowly growing light,
And shall become a new star burning bright.

Who is the saviour of this star of gold,
Like to that new-born Babe in times of old,
To whom they carried what they had to give
The hidden temple mysteries to retrieve?
They recognised Him in His earthly sheath,
The God who came to know and suffer death.

You bring Christ gold and frankincense and myrrh
That they as spirit gifts may know increase.
You bow your heads and will no longer err
And fall before Him gently on your knees.
You fold your hands, with hearts devout and humble,
And those who follow you will never stumble.

And though in Hell the demons did surround Him,
He finds the way to angel spheres above,
And even though all chaos were around Him,
From Him would flow a world of heavenly love.
For all the kings, all three, are there in you;
Three kings: the good, the beautiful, and true.

The Cross of the Dumb

FIONA MACLEOD

A Christmas on Iona, long, long ago.

One eve, when Saint Columba strode
In solemn mood along the shore,
He met an angel on the road
Who but a poor man's semblance bore.

He wondered much, the holy saint,
What stranger sought the lonely isle,
But seeing him weary and wan and faint
Saint Colum hailed him with a smile.

"Remote our lone Iona lies
Here in the grey and windswept sea,
And few are they whom my old eyes
Behold as pilgrims bowing the knee ...

But welcome ... welcome ... stranger-guest,
And come with me and you shall find
A warm and deer-skinn'd cell for rest
And at our board a welcome kind ...

Yet tell me ere the dune we cross
How came you to this lonely land?
No curraghs in the tideway toss
And none is beached upon the strand!"

The weary pilgrim raised his head
And looked and smiled and said, "From far,
My wandering feet have here been led
By the glory of a shining star ..."

Saint Colum gravely bowed, and said,
"Enough, my friend, I ask no more;
Doubtless some silence-vow was laid
Upon thee, ere thou sought'st this shore:

Now, come: and doff this raiment sad
And those rough sandals from thy feet:
The holy brethren will be glad
To haven thee in our retreat."

Together past the praying cells
And past the wattle-woven dome
Whence rang the tremulous vesper bells
Saint Colum brought the stranger home.

From thyme-sweet pastures grey with dews
The milch-cows came with swinging tails:
And whirling high, the wailing mews
Screamed o'er the brothers at their pails.

A single spire of smoke arose,
And hung, a phantom, in the cold:
Three younger monks set forth to close
The ewes and lambs within the fold.

The purple twilight stole above
The grey-green dunes, the furrowed leas:
And dusk, with breast as of a dove,
Brooded: and everwhere was peace.

Within the low refectory sate
The little clan of holy folk:
Then, while the brothers mused and ate,
The wayfarer arose and spoke ...

O Colum of Iona-Isle,
And ye who dwell in God's quiet place,
Before I crossed your narrow kyle
I looked in Heaven upon Christ's face.

Thereat Saint Colum's startled glance
Swept o'er the man so poorly clad,
And all the brethren looked askance
In fear the pilgrim-guest was mad. >>

And, Colum of God's Church i' the sea
And all ye Brothers of the Rood,
The Lord Christ gave a dream to me
And bade me bring it ye as food.

Lift to the wandering cloud your eyes
And let them scan the wandering Deep ...
Hark ye not there the wandering sighs
Of brethren ye as outcasts keep?

Thereat the stranger bowed, and blessed;
Then, grave and silent, sought his cell:
Saint Colum mused upon his guest,
Dumb wonder on the others fell.

At dead of night the Abbot came
To where the weary wayfarer slept:
"Tell me," he said "thy holy name ..."
— No more, for on bowed knees he wept ...

Great awe and wonder fell on him;
His mind was like a lonely wild
When suddenly is heard a hymn
Sung by a little innocent child.

For now he knew their guest to be
No man as he and his, but one
Who in the Courts of Ecstasy
Worships, flame-winged, the Eternal Son.

The poor bare cell was filled with light,
That came from the swung moons the Seven
Seraphim swing day and night
Adown the infinite walls of Heaven.

But on the fern-wove mattress lay
No weary guest. Saint Colum kneeled
And found no trace; but ashen-grey,
Far off he heard glad anthems pealed.

At sunrise when the matins-bell
Made a cold silvery music fall
Through silence of each lonely cell
And over every fold and stall,

Saint Colum called his monks to come
And follow him to where his hands
Would raise the Great Cross of the Dumb
Upon the Holy Island's sands ...

"For I shall call from out the Deep
And from the grey fields of the skies,
The brethren we as outcasts keep,
Our kindred of the dumb wild eyes ...

Behold, on this Christ's natal morn,
God wills the widening of His laws,
Another miracle to be born —
For lo, our guest an Angel was!

His Dream the Lord Christ gave to him
To bring to us as Christ-Day food,
That Dream shall rise a holy hymn
And hang like a flower upon the Rood!"

Thereat, while all with wonder stared
Saint Colum raised the Holy Tree:
Then all with Christ-Day singing fared
To where the last sands lipped the sea.

Saint Colum raised his arms on high ...
O ye, all creatures of the wing,
Come here from out the fields o' the sky
Come here and learn a wondrous thing.

At that the wild clans of the air
Came sweeping in a mist of wings —
Ospreys and fierce solanders there,
Sea-swallows wheeling mazy rings, >>

The foam-white mew, the green-black scart,
The famishing hawk, the wailing tern,
All birds from the sand-building mart
To lonely bittern and heron ...

Saint Colum raised beseeching hands
And blessed the pastures of the sea:
Come, all ye creatures, to the sands,
Come and behold the Sacred Tree!

At that the cold clans of the wave
With spray and surge and splash appeared:
Up from each wreck-strewn, lightless cave
Dim day-struck eyes affrighted peered.

The pollacks came with rushing haste,
The great sea-cod, the speckled bass;
Along the foaming tideway raced
The herring-tribes like shimmering glass:

The mackerel and the dog-fish ran,
The whiting, haddock, in their wake:
The great sea-flounders upward span,
The fierce-eyed conger and the hake:

The greatest and the least of these
From hidden pools and tidal ways
Surged in their myriads from the seas
And stared at Saint Columba's face.

"Hearken," he cried, with solemn voice —
"Hearken! ye people of the Deep,
Ye people of skies, Rejoice!
No more your soulless terror keep!

For lo, an Angel from the Lord
Hath shown us that wherein we sin —
But now we humbly do his Word
And call you, Brothers, kith and kin ...

No more we claim the world as ours
And everything that therein is —
Today, Christ's-Day, the infinite powers
Decree a common share of bliss.

I know not if the new-waked soul
That stirs in every heart I see
Has yet to reach the far-off goal
Whose symbol is this Cross-shaped Tree ...

But, O dumb kindred of the skies,
O kinsfolk of the pathless seas,
All scorn and hate I exorcise,
And wish you nought but Love and Peace!"

Thus, on that Christmas-day of old
Saint Colum broke the ancient spell.
A thousand years away have rolled,
'Tis now ... "a baseless miracle."

O fellow-kinsmen of the Deep,
O kindred of the wind and cloud,
God's children too ... how He must weep
Who on that day was glad and proud!

Snowflakes

DAVID KUHRT

Snowflakes
white as frozen light
where darkness dies
and heaven lies
incarnate on the ground.

To a Snowflake

FRANCIS THOMPSON

What heart could have thought you?
Past our devisal
(O filigree petal!)
Fashioned so purely,
Fragilely, surely
From what Paradisal
Imagineless metal
Too costly for cost?
Who hammered you, wrought you,
From argentine vapour?
"God was my shaper.
Passing surmisal,
He hammered, He wrought me,
From curled silver vapour,
To lust of His mind —
Thou couldst not have thought me!
So purely, so palely,
Tinily, surely,
Mightily, frailly,
Insculped and embossed,
With His hammer of wind
And His graver of frost."

From *Love's Labours Lost*

WILLIAM SHAKESPEARE

When icicles hang by the wall,
And Dick the shepherd blows his nail,
And Tom bears logs into the hall,
And milk comes frozen home in pail,
When blood is nipp'd, and ways be foul,
Then nightly sings the staring owl,
Tu-whit! Tu-who! A merry note!
While greasy Joan doth keel the pot.

When all about the wind doth blow,
And coughing drowns the parson's saw,
And birds sit brooding in the snow,
And Marian's nose looks red and raw;
When roasted crabs hiss in the bowl —
Then nightly sings the staring owl
Tu-whit! Tu-who! a merry note!
While greasy Joan doth keel the pot.

Jack Frost

CECILY E. PIKE

Look out! Look out!
Jack Frost is about!
He's after our fingers and toes;
And all through the night,
The gay little sprite
Is working where nobody knows.

He'll climb each tree,
So nimble is he,
His silvery powder he'll shake;
To windows he'll creep
And while we're asleep,
Such wonderful pictures he'll make.

Across the grass
He'll merrily pass,
And change all its greenness to white;
Then home he will go
And laugh "Ho, ho, ho,
What fun I have had in the night."

In the Wood

EILEEN MATHIAS

Cold winter's in the wood
I saw him pass —
Crinkling up fallen leaves
Along the grass —

Bleak winter's in the wood,
The birds have flown
Leaving the naked trees
Shivering alone.

King Winter's in the wood,
I saw him go —
Crowned with a coronet
Of crystal snow.

Outside

HUGH CHESTERMAN

King Winter sat in his Hall one day,
    And he said to himself, said he,
"I must admit I've had some fun,
I've chilled the earth and cooled the Sun,
    And not a flower or a tree
But wishes that my reign were done,
And as long as time and tide shall run,
I'll go on making everyone
As cold as cold can be."

There came a knock at the outer door:
    "Who's there?" King Winter cried;
"Open your palace gate," said Spring
For you can reign no more as King,
    Nor longer here abide;
This message from the Sun I bring,
"The trees are green, the birds do sing;
The hills with joy are echoing:
    So pray, Sir — step outside!"

Winter and Summer

ANONYMOUS

Winter creeps, nature sleeps,
Birds are gone, flowers are none;
Fields are bare, bleak the air,
Leaves are shed, all things dead;

God's alive, grow and thrive,
Hid away, bloom of May,
Rose of June. Very soon
Naught but green will be seen.

Spring and Easter

The Magic Piper

E.L. MARSH

There piped a piper in the wood
Strange music — soft and sweet —
And all the little wild things
Came hurrying to his feet.

They sat around him on the grass,
Enchanted, unafraid,
And listened, as with shining eyes
Sweet melodies he made.

The wood grew green, and flowers sprang up,
The birds began to sing;
For the music it was magic,
And the piper's name was — Spring!

Written in March

WILLIAM WORDSWORTH

The Cock is crowing,
The stream is flowing,
The small birds twitter,
The lake doth glitter,
The green field sleeps in the sun;
The oldest and youngest
Are at work with the strongest;
The cattle are grazing,
Their heads never raising;
There are forty feeding like one!

Like an army defeated
The snow hath retreated,
And now doth fare ill
On top of the bare hill;
The Ploughboy is whooping
— anon — anon:
There's joy in the mountains;
There's life in the fountains;
Small clouds are sailing,
Blue sky prevailing;
The rain is over and gone!

Longing for Spring

ANONYMOUS

Come, lovely May, with blossoms
And boughs of tender green,
And lead me over the meadows
Where cowslips first were seen.

For now I long to welcome
The radiant flowers of spring,
And through the wild woods wander,
And hear the sweet birds sing.

Spring Prayer

RALPH WALDO EMERSON

For flowers that bloom about our feet,
For tender grass so fresh and sweet,
For song of bird and hum of bee,
For all things fair we hear or see,
Father in Heaven, we thank thee!

For blue of streams and blue of sky,
For pleasant shade of branches high,
For fragrant air and cooling breeze,
For beauty of the blooming trees,
Father in heaven, we thank thee!

The Snowdrops

ANNIE MATHESON

"Where are all the snowdrops?" asked the sun
"Dead" said the frost "and buried every one."
"A foolish answer," said the sun,
"They did not die, asleep they lie
And I will wake them, I, the sun
Into the light, all clad in white
They shall grow every one."

The Snowdrop

CHRISTINA T. OWEN

I found a tiny snowdrop, blooming in the cold,
I'll share with you the secret the little flower told:
"Though winter still is here, it hasn't long to stay.
I came ahead to tell you that spring is on the way."

A Spring Poem

Snowdrops we, petals three, you may see.
White, green, gold, we unfold, in the cold.
Words of cheer speak we clear, spring is near.

Pippa's Song

ROBERT BROWNING

The year's at the spring,
The day's at the morn;
The morning's at seven;
The hillside's dew-pearled:
The lark's on the wing;
The snail's on the thorn;
God's in his heaven —
All's right with the world!

Spring Work at the Farm

THIRZA WAKLEY

What does the farmer do in the spring?
He sows the seed that harvests bring;
But first he wakes the earth from sleep
By ploughing it well and harrowing deep.

And busy must be the farmer's boy!
To care for the lambs that leap for joy.
To feed the calves so tender and young
He rises as soon as the day's begun.

And then the farmer's wife so kind,
Food for the ducklings and chicks will find.
And, hark! what the queer little piggy-wigs say,
"Don't forget me, I'm hungry today."

ANONYMOUS

A little bit of blowing
A little bit of snow
A little bit of growing
And crocuses will show.
On every twig that's lonely
A new green leaf will spring
On every patient tree-top
A thrush will stop and sing.

Little Green Finger

CHRISTINA T. OWEN

I looked in my garden and what did I see?
A little green finger that pointed at me!
It pointed at me from the spot where I know
I planted a little brown bulb long ago.

The little brown bulb so wrinkled and dry
Had pushed above ground, green leaves finger-high.
The leaves will grow taller, a bud will appear,
And soon I shall see a daffodil here.

Spring

ANONYMOUS

Sound the flute!
Now it's mute;
Birds delight
Day and night
Merrily, merrily to welcome in the year.

Nightingale
In the dale;
Lark in sky
Merrily, merrily to welcome in the year.

Song for Spring

JOAN WYLES

Glory be — glory be!
Every field, every tree
Comes to life, comes to leaf —
Gone Old Winter's ache and grief —
Come the Spring! Throstle sing!
Lamb in meadow leap and spring
Greet the Spring,
Hey ding-a-ding ding!

Spring Morning

ANONYMOUS

Now the moisty wood discloses
Wrinkled leaves of primroses,
While the birds they flute and sing:
"Build your nests, for here is spring!"

All about the open hills
Daisies show their pleasant frills,
Washed and white and newly spun
For a festival of sun.

Like a blossom from the sky,
Drops a yellow butterfly,
Dancing down the hedges grey
Snow-bestrewn till yesterday.

Squirrels skipping up the trees
Smell how spring is in the breeze,
While the birds, they flute and sing:
"Build your nests, for here is spring!"

Spring

MARION ATKINSON *(aged 11 years)*

Trees get back their leaves
And out come birds and bees;
Lambs bleat, children shout,
That's what spring is all about!

The Fairy Ring

ANONYMOUS

Let us dance and let us sing,
Dancing in a merry ring,
We'll be fairies on the green
Sporting round the fairy queen.

Like the seasons of the year
Round we circle in a sphere.
I'll be summer, you'll be spring
Dancing in a fairy ring.

Spring and summer glide away,
Autumn comes with tresses gay.
Winter hand in hand with spring
Dancing in a fairy ring.

Faster, faster round we go,
While our cheeks with roses glow,
Free as birds upon the wing
Dancing in a fairy ring.

Spring Poem

Waken, sleeping butterfly,
Burst your narrow prison.
Spread your golden wings and fly
For the sun is risen!
Spread your wings and tell the story
How He rose, the King of Glory.

A Spring Song

ANONYMOUS

See the yellow catkins cover
All the slender willows over;
And on the mossy banks so green
Starlike primroses are seen;
And their clustering leaves below
White and purple violets grow.

Hark, the little lambs are bleating
And the cawing rooks are meeting
In the elms, a noisy crowd;
And all birds are singing loud.
There, the first white butterfly
In the sun goes flitting by.

The Bells of Youth

FIONA MACLEOD

The Bells of Youth are ringing in the gateways of the South:
    The bannerets of green are now unfurled:
Spring has risen with a laugh, a wild-rose in her mouth,
    And is singing, singing, singing thro' the world.

The Bells of Youth are ringing in all the silent places,
    The primrose and the celandine are out:
Children run a-laughing with joy upon their faces,
    The west wind follows after with a shout.

The Bells of Youth are ringing from the forests to the mountains,
    From the meadows to the moorlands, hark their ringing!
Ten thousand thousand splashing rills and fern-dappled fountains
    Are flinging wide the Song of Youth, and onward flowing, singing!

The Bells of Youth are ringing in the gateways of the South:
    The bannerets of green are now unfurled:
Spring has risen with a laugh, a wild-rose in her mouth,
    And is singing, singing, singing thro' the world.

Resurgence

DAVID KUHRT

Resurgent in every vein and pore the spring
beneath the black and hardened frame of winter
burgeons. Winter gives urgent ground
to stirring worms, who crumble inexorably the dark.
Daffodils appear. The light is come full term.

A fine chemistry of sense accommodates rebirth
and now this disencumbered world attends
the audible demand of your sweet tongue.
Formal and articulate it bends again
to enter, shaped in these words.

A Hymn for Easter Day

EDMUND SPENSER

Most glorious Lord of Lyfe, that, on this day,
Didst make Thy triumph over death and sin,
And, having harrowed hell, didst bring away
Captivity thence captive, us to win:
This joyous day, deare Lord, with joy begin;
And grant that we, for whom thou diddest dye,
Being with Thy deare blood clene washt from sin,
May live for ever in felicity!
And that Thy love we weighing worthily,
May likewise love Thee for the same againe;
And for Thy sake, that all lyke deare didst buy,
With love may one another entertayne!
    So let us love, deare Love, lyke as we ought,
    Love is the lesson which the Lord us taught.

Easter

FIONA MACLEOD

The stars wailed when the reed was born
And heaven wept at the birth of the thorn;
Joy was plucked like a flower and torn,
For Time pre-shadowed Good-Friday morn.

But the stars laughed like children free
And heaven was hung with the rainbow's glee
When on Easter Sunday, so fair to see,
Time bowed before Eternity.

From *Five Easters*

ANASTASIUS GRÜN

Though known to none, yet with its ancient blessing,
Eternal in their breast it stands upright;
There blooms its seed abroad on every pathway,
A Cross it was — this stranger to their sight.

The Cross of Stone now stands within a garden,
A strange and sacred relic from old;
Flowers of all patterns lift their growth above it,
While roses, climbing high, the Cross enfold.

So stood the Cross, weighty with solemn meaning,
On Golgotha, amidst resplendent sheen.
Long since 'tis hidden by its sheath of roses;
No more, for roses, can the cross be seen.

Easter

DAVID KUHRT

Remember the sacrifice to the trees
and break off with care a small bouquet of leaves.
Take indoors the great countryside!
Between the breaking buds a few bright
roundnesses prick out the crumbled bark —
such tiny corbels underpin that edifice of light and dark.

Resurrection

FOURTEENTH CENTURY

Wintertide hath passed away,
Now Christ the Lord is ris'n today
All Christendom to cheer:
See the meads with flow'rets sheen!
Spring hath thawed rill and mere,
Larks are singing, woods are green,
Life with Christ doth reappear.

An Easter Greeting

MARTHA G.D. BIANCHI
Translated from the Russian

The lark at sunrise trills it high
The greeting: Christ is risen!
And through the wood the blackbird pipes
The greeting: Christ is risen!
Beneath the eaves the swallows cry
The greeting: Christ is risen!
Throughout the world man's heart proclaims
The greeting: Christ is risen.
An echo answers from the grave:
In truth, yes, He is risen.

An Easter Wish

TRADITIONAL

May the glad dawn
Of Eastern morn
Bring joy to thee.

May the calm eve
Of Easter leave
A peace divine with thee.

May Easter night
On thine heart write
O Christ, I live for Thee.

Easter Poem

J.M. NEALE

Let the merry Church bells ring
Hence with tears and sighing
Frost and cold have fled from Spring
Life hath conquered dying.

Flowers are smiling, fields are gay,
Sunny is the weather
With our rising Lord today
All things rise together!

Days grow longer, sunbeams stronger
Easter tide makes all things new;
Lent is banished, sadness vanished
Christ has risen, rise we too.

May

ANONYMOUS

The little birds have burst their shells
With hungry beaks they cry;
Their busy parents bring them food
And teach them how to fly.

Small twittering finches fill the hedge
And rooks the elm-trees tall
The wagtails run about the lawn
And whistling blackbirds call.

Fat pigeons coo in warm content
Slim swallows dart and play
The thrushes sweetly sing at dusk
And cuckoos shout all day.

Song: On May Morning

JOHN MILTON

Now the bright morning star, day's harbinger,
Comes dancing from the east, and leads with her
The flow'ry May, who from her green lap throws
The yellow cowslip and the pale primrose.
Hail, bounteous May, thou dost inspire
Mirth and youth and warm desire!
Woods and groves are of thy dressing,
Hill and dale doth boast thy blessing.
Thus we salute thee with our early song,
And welcome thee, and wish thee long.

In May I Go a-Walking

FOLK SONG

In May I go a-walking
To hear the linnet sing,
The blackbird and the throstle
A-praising God the King.

It cheers the heart to hear them
To see the leaves unfold
The meadows covered over
With buttercups of gold.

Hymn for Whitsun

AMBROSIUS

Image of our Father's spendour,
Streaming light from light divine,
Light of light, fountain of radiance,
As Day the illuminator of day,
You true Sun, bend down,
Overflowing with eternal glory
And pour the holy spirit's flood
Deep into the senses' chalice.

Summer

Sunflowers

HEATHER THOMAS

Sunflowers in the summer growing,
Growing up towards the light;
Light and warmth which draws them upwards,
Upwards striving in their might.

Mighty golden heads with seeds there,
Seeds to sleep in winter's ground;
Heads which turn from dawn till sunset
Following the sun's path round.

Song for St John's Fire

ALFRED CECIL HARWOOD

Now the high midsummer sun
Burns the dreaming hours away,
Kindles blossoms bright as flames,
Flashes light from leaf and spray.

Light is quivering on the moor,
Air is hot with honeyed smells,
Golden rivers burn and glide,
Shining brooks are singing spells.

Butterflies like flowers a-wing,
Tremble as they drink the light,
Golden pollen fills the sky,
Downy seeds soar out of sight.

When the traveller sun goes home,
And stars come slowly overhead,
Ling'ring lustres track him round
Till the flush of dawn is red.

Earth and Man, have you no fire
To greet these heaven-kindled hours?
Earth has fire, and hearts have fire —
Light the flame among the flowers!

History

From *King Olaf*

HENRY WADSWORTH LONGFELLOW

Interlude

And then the blue-eyed Norseman told
A Saga of the days of old.
"There is," said he, "a wondrous book
Of Legends in the old Norse tongue,
Of the dead kings of Norroway,
Legends that once were told or sung
In many a smoky fireside nook
Of Iceland, in the ancient day,
By wandering Saga-man or Scald;
Heimskringla is the volume called;
And he who looks may find therein
The story that I now begin."

And in each pause the story made
Upon his violin he played,
As an appropriate interlude,
Fragments of old Norwegian tunes
That bound in one the separate runes,
And held the mind in perfect mood,
Entwining and encircling all
The strange and antiquated rhymes
With melodies of olden times,

As over some half-ruined wall,
Disjointed and about to fall,
Fresh woodbines climb and interlace,
And keep the loosened stones in place.

I am the God Thor,
I am the War God,
I am the Thunderer!
Here in my Northland,
My fastness and fortress,
Reign I forever!

Here amid icebergs
Rule I the nations;
This is my hammer,
Miölner the mighty;
Giants and sorcerers
Cannot withstand it!

These are the gauntlets
Wherewith I wield it,
And hurl it afar off.
This is my girdle;
Whenever I brace it,
Strength is redoubled!

The light thou beholdest
Stream through the heavens,
In flashes of crimson,
Is but my red beard
Blown by the night-wind,
Affrighting the nations!

Jove is my brother;
Mine eyes are the lightning;
The wheels of my chariot
Roll in the thunder,
The blows of my hammer
Ring in the earthquake!

Force rules the world still;
Has ruled it, shall rule it;
Meekness is weakness,
Strength is triumphant,
Over the whole earth
Still it is Thor's-Day!

Thou art a God too,
O Galilean!
And thus single-handed
Unto the combat,
Gauntlet or Gospel,
Here I defy thee!

Indian Poem

Every moment the voice of love comes from left and right,
But here on earth is darkness, grant us eternal light.
We have lived in heaven, the angels were our friends,
Thither let us go, for there our suffering ends.

The Creation

Genesis

Breshit bara Elohim
Et hashamaim w'et ha'aretz.
Weha'aretz haita tohoo wabohoo
Wachoshech al-pney tahoom
Waroo'ach Elohim merachefetz
Al-pney hamaim
Wayomer Elohim
Yehi ohr, wayehi ohr.
Wayerah Elohim
Et-ha'ohr ki-tov
Wayavdel Elohim
Bin ha'ohr oobin hachoshech
Wayikrah Elohim l'ohr yom
W'lachoshech karah lailah
Weyehee-erev, weyehee-boker
Yom echad.

בראשית ברא אלהים
את השמים ואת הארץ:
והארץ היתה תהו ובהו
וחשך על־פני תהום
ורוח אלהים מרחפת
על־פני המים:
ויאמר אלהים
יהי אור ויהי־אור:
וירא אלהים
את־האור כי־טוב
ויבדל אלהים
בין האור ובין החשך:
ויקרא אלהים לאור יום
ולחשך קרא לילה
ויהי־ערב ויהי־בקר
יום אחד:

In the beginning God created
The heavens and the earth
And the earth was without form and void
And darkness ruled on the face of the depths.
And the spirit of God brooded
On the face of the waters.
And God said
Let there be light, and there was light
And God saw
that the light was good,
And God separated
the light and the darkness
And God called the the light, day,
And the darkness he called night,
And there was evening and there was morning
One day.

Song of Creation

FROM *THE RIG VEDA*

Nasad asin, na sad asit tadanim:
Nasid rajo no vioma paro yat.
Kim avarivah? Kuha? Kasya sarmann?
Amba kim asid, gahanam gabithram?

Translation:
There was not non-existent nor existent:
There was no realm of air, no sky beyond it.
What covered in and where? And what gave shelter?
Was water there, unfathomed depth of water?

From *Chapters from Ancient History*

DOROTHY HARRER

Ancient India

[*The whole Veda is the first source of the sacred law. Whatever law has been ordained for any person by Manu, that has been fully declared in the* VEDA.
BRAHMANS: Priests, leaders of science and religion.
KSHATRIYAS: Kings, warriors, administrators.
VAISYAS: Farmers, merchants, craftsmen.
SUDRAS: Duty to serve others.]

Rich in royal worth and valour,
Rich in holy Vedic lore,
Dasaratha ruled his empire
In the happy days of yore —

Like the ancient monarch Manu,
Father of the human race,
Dasaratha ruled his people
With a father's loving grace — >>

Twice-born men were free from passion,
Lust of gold and impure greed,
Faithful to their rites and scriptures,
Truthful in their word and deed —

Kshatriyas bowed to holy Brahmans,
Vaisyas to Kshatriyas bowed,
Toiling Sudras lived by labour
Of their honest duty proud.

Ancient Persia

In the flaming fire we worship thee,
Master of Wisdom,
Lord of Light,
AHURA-MAZDA,
O Spirit speak to us
In the glory of the Sun,
O Lord of Life.

From the regions of the North,
From the regions of the South,
Forth rushed Ahriman the deadly,
And the demons of darkness, the evil-doers;
Thus spake Ahriman, the deadly Deceiver:
"Kill him, destroy him, Hated Zarathustra."

Thus spake Zarathustra:
"The world of AHURA-MAZDA is my weapon,
With his sword will I strike
The Holy word of the Lord of Light,
The living word of Creation."
Forth fled Ahriman, the Deceiver,
And the wicked evil-doing Demons
Into the depths of outer darkness.

Ancient Egypt: Hymn to the Sun

Open the gates of the East and the West
Open the gates of the South and the North!
For the boat of the Sunset goes to its rest
And the boat of the Daybreak waits to come forth.

Open your gates, O ye Regions of Night!
Let the Boat of the Dawn sail your pillars between,
Let the Abd-fish disport him in ripples of light,
And in eddies of turquoise the Ynt-fish be seen.

Gold is the river, the Nile of the sky,
Flashing with gold comes the Boat of the Dawn.
Shrine of the South, lift your portals on high!
Shrine of the North, let your bolts be withdrawn!

Serpent of Baklu, why sleepest thou still?
Wake! for the darkness is passing away.
Wake! for the dawn-light is flooding the hill
As the Boat of the Morning speeds to the day.

Fling wide the gates of the East and the West
Wide are the gates of the South and the North!
For the Boat of the Sunset has passed to its rest
And the Boat of the Sunrise hastes to come forth!

He Knoweth the Souls of the West

FROM *THE BOOK OF THE DEAD*

High on the Mountain of Sunrise where standeth the Temple of Sebek
There lieth a Serpent of flint and glistening plates of metal
His name is the Dweller in Fire, and he is the foe of the Morning,
He stoppeth the Boat of Ra, and wrappeth the Boatmen in slumber.
But he shall be held in restraint and the Boat of Ra sail onward,
Yea, I am the Man who restraineth the Serpent with mighty enchantment
And fettereth the foe of the Sunrise till Ra resume the horizon.
I, even I, have fettered him, and greeted the souls of the West,
The Lord of the Mountain of Sunset, and Hathor, the Lady of Evening.

Hymn to Osiris

Shout aloud, ye people who within the temple stand,
    Glory to omnipotent Osiris!
Blazen forth his triumph till his splendour fills the land,
    Honour to the living God, Osiris!

Secret is his nature, and his ways beyond our ken,
    Ancient, yet a babe, is great Osiris;
As the Moon he watches and divides the months for men,
    Times and seasons wait upon Osiris.

When the Sun-god passes to the realm of Death and Night,
    Monarch of that kingdom is Osiris;
When he comes in glory in the glowing morning-light,
    Throned on high beside him is Osiris.

When the river rises bringing happiness and mirth,
    As the joyous Nile we hail Osiris;
Giver of the harvest and Creator of the earth,
    All we have and are is from Osiris.

Women, hymn his triumph; let your voices, men, ring out;
    Cry aloud, all creatures of Osiris!
Thunder forth his praises in one vast triumphant shout,
    Glory to the risen Lord, Osiris!

Hymn of Praise to Ra

FROM *THE BOOK OF THE DEAD*

Beautiful is Thy awakening
    Thou hawk of the morning
Thou glorious Being
    That openest Thine eyes
Thou lofty Being
    Whose course is not known to man
Thou image great
    The horizon's first born.

Exceedingly high Thou art
    And beyond man's reach
That risest from the ocean as a bird
    That drivest away darkness
And bringest light
    He overcometh the Serpent of Evil
In the name of Ra.

Akhnaten's Hymn to Aton

When thou risest in the eastern horizon of heaven
    Thou fillest every land with thy beauty.
When thou settest in the western horizon of heaven
    The world is in darkness and as dead,
Bright is the earth when thou risest in the horizon,
    When thou shinest as Aton by day,
The darkness is banished when thou sendest forth thy rays.
    How manifold are thy works,
    They are hidden from before us.
O thou one God, whose powers no other possesseth.
Thou didst create the world according to thy word
    While thou wast alone.
    By thee men live.
    The world is in thy hands
    And thou art in my heart
    For thou thyself art the life of time.
    By thee men live
    Until thou settest;
    Thou makest the beauty of form,
    Thou art in my heart.

Egyptian Hymn to the Sun

Homage to Thee O Ra — at thy tremendous rising
Thou risest, thou shinest, the heavens are rolled aside —
Thou art the King of Gods, thou art the all-comprising
From Thee we come, in Thee are deified.

Thy rays are upon all faces — thou art inscrutable
Age after age thy life renews its eager prime —
Time whirls its dust beneath thee,
Thou art immutable —
Maker of Time, thyself beyond all time.

Thou passest thro' the portals that close behind the night
Gladdening the souls of them that lie in sorrow.
The true of word, the quiet heart arise and drink thy light,
Thou art today and yesterday, thou art tomorrow.

Homage to Thee O Ra, who wakest life from slumber —
Thou risest, thou shinest, thy radiant face appears —
Millions of years have passed — we cannot count their number —
Millions of years shall come — Thou art beyond the years!

The Destruction of Sennacherib

GEORGE GORDON, LORD BYRON

The Assyrian came down like the wolf on the fold,
And his cohorts were gleaming in purple and gold;
And the sheen of their spears was like stars on the sea,
When the blue wave rolls nightly on deep Galilee.

Like the leaves of the forest when Summer is green,
That host with their banners at sunset were seen:
Like the leaves of the forest when Autumn hath blown,
That host on the morrow lay wither'd and strown.

For the Angel of Death spread his wings on the blast,
And breathed in the face of the foe as he pass'd;
And the eyes of the sleepers wax'd deadly and chill,
And their hearts but once heaved, and for ever grew still!

And there lay the steed with his nostril all wide,
But through it there roll'd not the breath of his pride;
And the foam of his gasping lay white on the turf,
And cold as the spray of the rock-beating surf.

And there lay the rider distorted and pale,
With the dew on his brow, and the rust on his mail:
And the tents were all silent, the banners alone,
The lances unlifted, the trumpet unblown.

And the widows of Ashur are loud in their wail,
And the idols are broke in the temple of Baal;
And the might of the Gentile, unsmote by the sword,
Hath melted like snow in the glance of the Lord!

From *Vision of Belshazzar*

GEORGE GORDON, LORD BYRON

The King was on his throne,
    The Satraps* throng'd the hall:
A thousand bright lamps shone
    O'er that high festival.
A thousand cups of gold,
    In Judah deem'd divine —
Jehovah's vessels hold
    The godless Heathen's wine!

In that same hour and hall,
    The fingers of a hand
Came forth against the wall,
    And wrote as if on sand:

>>

* Satrap, a provisional governor in ancient Persia.

The fingers of a man; —
 A solitary hand
Along the letters ran,
 And traced them like a wand.

The monarch saw, and shook,
 And bade no more rejoice;
All bloodless wax'd his look,
 And tremulous his voice.
"Let the men of lore appear,
 The wisest of the earth,
And expound the words of fear,
 Which mar our royal mirth."

Chaldea's seers are good,
 But here they have no skill;
And the unknown letters stood
 Untold and awful still.
And Babel's men of age
 Are wise and deep in lore;
But now they were not sage,
 They saw — but knew no more.

A captive in the land,
 A stranger and a youth,
He heard the king's command,
 He saw that writing's truth.
The Lamps around were bright,
 The prophecy in view;
He read it on that night —
 The morrow proved it true.

"Belshazzar's grave is made,
 His kingdom pass'd away,
He, in the balance weigh'd,
 Is light and worthless clay;
The shroud his robe of state,
 His canopy the stone;
The Mede is at his gate!
 The Persian on his throne!"

The Prologue to the Gospel of St John

᾽Εν ἀρχη ἠν ὁ λογος,
και ὁ λογος ἠν προς τον θεον,
και θεος ἠν ὁ λογος.
Οὑτος ἠν ἐν ἀρχη προς τον θεον.
Παντα δι αὐτου ἐγενετο,
και χωρις αὐτου ἐγενετο οὐδε ἐν ὁ γεγονεν.
᾽Εν αὐτω ζωη ἠν,
και ἡ ζωη ἠν το φως των ἀνθρωπων.
και το φως ἐν σκοτια φαινει,
και ἡ σκοτια αὐτο οὐ κατελαβεν.

Translation:
In the beginning was the Word,
and the Word was with God,
and God was the Word.
The same was in the beginning with God.
All things were made by him;
and without him was not anything made that was made.
In him was Light;
and the life was the Light of men.
And the light shines in the darkness;
and the darkness comprehended it not.

Ancient Greece

Zeus

HOMER

He whose all-conscious eyes the world behold,
The eternal thunderer sat, enthroned in gold;
High heaven the footstool of his feet he makes
And wide beneath him all Olympus shakes.

Hexameter

ANONYMOUS

Then on the brow of the maiden
 a veil bound Pallas Athene,
Ample it fell to her feet,
 deep fringed, a wonder of weaving.
Ages and ages agone
 it was wrought on the heights of Olympus,
Wrought on the gold string loom
 by the finger of cunning Athene
In it she wove all creatures
 that team in the womb of the ocean,
Nereid, Siren and Triton,
 and dolphin and silvery fishes
Glittering round many hued
 on the flame red folds of the mantle.

Hercules

EILEEN HUTCHINS

Who is this who cometh as in conquest?
 Strong he strides and free.
Light of glory gleams around his temples,
 More than man is he.

Dark has been the danger of his daring,
 Fierce the first and fell;
None can know the fashion of his faring
 Hither out of hell.

Who is this who cometh as in conquest?
 Strong he strides and free.
Light of glory gleams around his temples,
 Man and god is he.

Hymn to Prometheus

ROY WILKINSON

Hail to Prometheus, the Titan,
 the helper of man and creator.
Clay was the substance he used
 and in likeness of gods then he shaped it.
Goodness and evil from hearts
 of the beasts in man's breast he enfolded.
Fire he brought down from the realms
 of the skies to perfect his creation.
Movement of stars he explained
 to the wondering earth dwelling people.
Numbers he taught them to use
 and the plants which heal sickness he showed them.
Symbols he taught them to write,
 representing the sounds of their speaking.
Building of ships he did teach
 and the training of beasts to man's service.
Into the depths of the earth
 did he guide men to find precious metals.
Zeus he defied and brought fire
 down again when the god would deny men.
Torment and anguish he suffered
 for harsh was the fate decreed for him.
Bound to a cliff overhanging
 a sinister cleft was Prometheus.
Bravely the Titan endured
 and at length one arrived to release him.

Roma

O Roma nobilis,	O noble Rome,
Orbis et domina.	The circle and mistress.
Omnium urbium,	Of all cities,
Excellentissima.	Most excellent.
Salutem dicimus	We give greetings
Tibi per omnia;	To you among all:
Te benedicimus,	To you we give blessing,
Salve per saecula.	Salute through the year.

Pater Noster

THE LORD'S PRAYER IN LATIN

Pater noster, qui es in caelis,
Sanctificetur nomen tuum.
Adveniat regnum tuum.
Fiat voluntas tua, sicut in caelis et in terra.
Panem nostrum quotidianum da nobis hodie.
Et dimitte nobis debita nostra,
Sicut et nostra dimittimus debitoribus nostris.
Et ne nos inducas in tentationem.
Sed libera nos a malo.
Amen.

From *Horatius Keeps the Bridge*

LORD MACAULAY

Out spake the Consul roundly:
"The bridge must straight go down;
For, since Janiculum is lost,
Nought else can save the town."
Then out spake brave Horatius,
The captain of the gate:
"To every man upon this earth
Death cometh soon or late.

And how can man die better
    Than facing fearful odds,
For the ashes of his fathers,
    And the temples of his gods?

And for the tender mother
    Who dandled him to rest,
And for the wife who nurses
    His baby at her breast,
And for the holy maidens
    Who feed the eternal flame,
To save them from false Sextus
    That wrought the deed of shame?

Hew down the bridge, Sir Consul,
    With all the speed you may;
I, with two more to help me,
    Will hold the foe in play.
In yon straight path a thousand
    May well be stopped by three.
Now, who will stand on either hand,
    And keep the bridge with me?"

Then out spake Spurius Lartius;
    A Ramnian proud was he;
"Lo, I will stand at thy right hand,
    And keep the bridge with thee."
And out spake strong Herminius.
    Of Titian blood was he:
"I will abide on thy left side,
    And keep the bridge with thee."

"Horatius," quoth the Consul,
    "As thou say'st, so let it be."
And straight against that great array
    Forth went the dauntless Three.
For Romans in Rome's quarrel
    Spared neither land nor gold,
Nor son nor wife, nor limb nor life,
    In the brave days of old.

>>

Then none was for a party;
Then all were for the state;
Then the great man helped the poor,
And the poor man loved the great;
Then lands were fairly portioned;
Then spoils were fairly sold;
The Romans were like brothers
In the brave days of old.

Now Roman is to Roman
More hateful than a foe,
And the tribunes bear the high
And the fathers grind the low.
As we wax hot in faction,
In battle we wax cold;
Wherefore men fight not as they fought
In the brave days of old.

Now while the Three were tightening
The harness on their backs,
The Consul was the foremost man
To take in hand an axe;
And fathers mixed with commons,
Seized hatchet bar, and crow,
And smote upon the planks above,
And loosed the props below.

Meanwhile the Tuscan army,
Right glorious to behold,
Came flashing back the noonday light,
Rank behind rank, like surges bright
Of a broad sea of gold.
Four hundred trumpets sounded
A peal of warlike glee,
As that great host with measured tread,
And spears advanced, and ensigns spread,
Rolled slowly towards the bridge's head,
Where stood the dauntless Three.

The Three stood calm and silent,
    And looked upon the foes,
And a great shout of laughter
    From all the vanguard rose;
And forth the Three came spurring
    Before that deep array,
To earth they sprang, their swords they drew,
    And lifted their shields, and flew
To win the narrow way.

Aunus, from green Tifernum,
    Lord of the Hill of Vines;
And Sieus, whose eight hundred slaves
    Sicken in Ilva's mines,
And Picus, long to Clusium
    Vassal in peace and war,
Who led to fight his Umbrian powers
    From that great crag where, girt with towers,
The fortress of Nequinum lowers,
    O'er the pale waves of Nar.

Stout Lartius hurled down Aunus
    Into the stream beneath;
Herminius struck at Seius,
    And clove him to the teeth:
At Picus brave Horatius
    Darted one fiery thrust;
And the proud Umbrian's gilded arms
    Clashed in the bloody dust.

Then all Etruria's noblest
    Felt their hearts sick to see
On the earth the bloody corpses,
    In the path the dauntless Three:
And, from this ghastly entrance
    Where those bold Romans stood,
All shrank, like boys who unaware,
    Ranging the woods to start a hare,
Come to the mouth of the dark lair,
    Where, growling low, a fierce old bear
Lies amidst bones and blood.

>>

Was none who would be foremost
 To lead such dire attack;
But those behind cried "Forward!"
 And those before cried "Back!"
And backward now and forward
 Wavers the deep array;
And on the tossing sea of steel,
 To and fro the standards reel;
And the victorious trumpet-peal
 Dies fitfully away.

But meanwhile axe and lever
 Have manfully been plied;
And now the bridge lies tottering
 Above the boiling tide.
"Come back, come back, Horatius!"
 Loud cried the fathers all,
"Back Lartius! Back Herminius!
 Back, ere the ruin fall!"

Back darted Spurius Lartius,
 Herminius darted back:
And, as they passed, beneath their feet
 They felt the timbers crack.
But when they turned their faces,
 And on the farther shore
Saw brave Horatius stand alone,
 They would have crossed once more.

But with a crash like thunder
 Fell every loosened beam,
And, like a dam, the mighty wreck
 Lay right athwart the stream:
And a long shout of triumph
 Rose from the walls of Rome,
As to the highest turret-tops
 Was splashed the yellow foam.

And, like a horse unbroken,
When first he feels the rein,
The furious river struggled hard,
And tossed his tawny mane,
And burst the curb, and bounded,
Rejoicing to be free,
And whirling down in fierce career,
Battlement, and plank, and pier,
Rushed headlong to the sea.

Alone stood brave Horatius,
But constant still in mind;
Thrice thirty thousand foes before,
And the broad flood behind.
"Down with him!" cried false Sextus,
With a smile on his pale face.
"Now yield thee!" cried Lars Porsena,
"Now yield thee to our grace."

Round turned he, as not deigning
Those craven ranks to see;
Nought spake he to Lars Porsena
To Sextus nought spake he;
But he saw on Palatinus
The white porch of his home;
And he spoke to the noble river,
That rolls by the towers of Rome,

"Oh, Tiber! Father Tiber!
To whom the Romans pray,
A Roman's life, a Roman's arms,
Take them in charge this day!"
So he spake and speaking sheathed
The good sword by his side,
And, with his harness on his back,
Plunged headlong in the tide.

No sound of joy or sorrow
Was heard from either bank;

>>

But friends and foes in dumb surprise,
With panting lips and straining eyes,
Stood gazing where he sank;
And when above the surges
They saw his crest appear,
All Rome sent forth a rapturous cry,
And even the ranks of Tuscany
Could scarce forbear to cheer.

But fiercely ran the current,
Swollen high by months of rain;
And fast his blood was flowing,
And he was sore in pain,
And heavy with his armour,
And spent with changing blows;
And oft they thought him sinking
But still again he rose.

Never, I ween, did swimmer,
In such an evil case,
Struggle through such a raging flood
Safe to the landing place;
But his limbs were born up bravely
By the brave heart within,
And our good Father Tiber
Bare bravely up his chin.

"Curse on him!" quoth false Sextus,
"Will not the villain drown?
But for this stay, ere close of day
We should have sacked the town!"
"Heaven help him!" quoth Lars Porsena,
"And bring him safe to shore,
For such a gallant feat of arms
Was never seen before."

And now he feels the bottom;
Now on dry earth he stands;

Now round him throng the Fathers
To press his gory hands;
And now with shouts and clapping,
And noise of weeping loud,
He enters through the River-Gate,
Borne by the joyous crowd.

They gave him of the corn-land,
That was of public right,
As much as two strong oxen
Could plough from morn till night:
And they made a molten image,
And set it up on high,
And there it stands unto the day
To witness if I lie.

It stands in the Comitium,
Plain for all folk to see;
Horatius in his harness,
Halting upon one knee:
And underneath is written,
In letters all of gold,
How valiantly he kept the bridge
In the brave days of old.

And still his name sounds stirring
Unto the men of Rome,
As the trumpet-blast that cries to them
To charge the Volscian home:
And wives still pray to Juno
For boys with hearts as bold
As his who kept the bridge so well
In the brave days of old.

And in the nights of winter,
When the cold north winds blow,
And the long howling of the wolves
Is heard amidst the snow;

>>

When round the lonely cottage
    Roars loud the tempest's din,
And the good logs of Algidus
    Roar louder yet within;

When the oldest cask is opened,
    And the largest lamp is lit,
When the chestnuts glow in embers
    And the kid turns on the spit;
When young and old in circle
    Around the firebrands close;
When the girls are weaving baskets,
    And the lads are shaping bows;

When the goodman mends his armour,
    And trims his helmet's plume;
When the goodwife's shuttle merrily
    Goes flashing through the loom:
With weeping and with laughter
    Still is the story told,
How well Horatius kept the bridge
    In the brave days of old.

Hymn to Diana

BEN JONSON

Queen and huntress, chaste and fair,
Now the sun is laid to sleep,
Seated, in thy silver chair,
State in wonted manner keep:
    Hesperus entreats thy light,
    Goddess, excellently bright.

Earth, let not thy envious shade
Dare itself to interpose;
Cynthia's shining orb was made
Heaven to clear, when day did close:
    Bless us then with wishèd sight,
    Goddess, excellently bright.

Lay thy bow of pearl apart,
And thy crystal-shining quiver;
Give unto the flying hart
Space to breathe, how short soever:
Thou, that mak'st a day of night,
Goddess, excellently bright!

From *The Passing of Arthur*

ALFRED, LORD TENNYSON

Then quickly rose Sir Bedivere, and ran,
And, leaping down the ridges lightly, plunged
Among the bulrush beds, and clutch'd the sword,
And strongly wheeled and threw it. The great brand
Made lightnings in the splendour of the moon,
And flashing round and round, and whirled in an arch,
Shot like a streamer of the northern morn,
Seen where the moving isles of winter shock
By night, with noises of the Northern Sea.
So flashed and fell the brand Excalibur:
But ere he dipt the surface, rose an arm
Clothed in white samite, mystic, wonderful,
And caught him by the hilt, and brandished him
Three times, and drew him under in the mere.
And lightly went the other to the King.

The War-Song of the Vikings

FIONA MACLEOD

Let loose the hounds of war,
The whirling swords!
Send them leaping afar,
Red in their thirst for war;
Odin laughs in his car
At the screaming of the swords!

>>

Far let the white-ones fly,
The whirling swords!
Afar off the ravens spy
Death-shadows cloud the sky.
Let the wolves of the Gael die
'Neath the screaming swords!

The Shining Ones yonder
High in Valhalla
Shout now, with thunder:
Drive the Gaels under,
Cleave them asunder —
Swords of Valhalla!

Norman and Saxon

RUDYARD KIPLING

"My son," said the Norman Baron,
"I am dying and you will be heir
To all the broad acres in England
that William gave me for my share
When we conquered the Saxon at Hastings,
and a nice little handful it is.
But before you go over to rule it
I want you to understand this:
The Saxon is not like us Normans.
His manners are not so polite,
But he never means anything serious
till he talks about justice and right.
When he stands like an ox in the furrow
with his sullen eyes set on your own,
And grumbles, 'This isn't fair dealing,'
my son, leave the Saxon alone."

"You can horsewhip your Gascony archers
or torture your Picardy spears;
But don't try that game on the Saxon;
you'll have the whole brood round your ears.

From the richest old Thane in the country
    to the poorest chained serf in the field,
They'll be at you and on you like hornets,
    and, if you are wise, you will yield."

"But first you must master their language,
    their dialect, proverbs and songs.
Don't trust any clerk to interpret
    when they come with the tale of their wrongs.
Let them know that you know what they're saying,
    let them feel that you know what to say.
Yes, even when you want to go hunting,
    hear 'em out if it takes you all day.
They'll drink every hour of the daylight
    and poach every hour of the dark.
It's the sport not the rabbits they're after
    (we've plenty of game in the park).
Dont hang them or cut off their fingers.
    That's wasteful as well as unkind
For a hard-bitten South-country poacher
    makes the best men-at-arms you can find.
Appear with your wife and the children
    at their weddings and funerals and feasts.
Be polite but not friendly to Bishops;
    be good to all poor parish priests.
Say 'we,' 'us' and 'ours' when you're talking,
    instead of 'you fellows' and 'I.'
Dont ride over seeds; keep your temper,
    and *never you tell 'em a lie!"*

King John and the Abbot of Canterbury

PERCY RELIQUES

An ancient story I'll tell you anon.
Of a notable prince, that was called King John:
And he ruled England with maine and with might,
For he did great wrong, and maintain'd little right. >>

And I'll tell you a story, a story so merrye,
Concerning the Abbot of Canterburye;
How for his housekeeping, and high renowne,
They rode poste for him to fair London towne.

An hundred men, the king did heare say,
The abbot kept in his house every day;
And fifty gold chaynes, without any doubt,
In velvet coates waited the abbot about.

"How now, father abbot I heare it of thee,
Thou keepest a farre bener house than me,
And for thy housekeeping and high renowne,
I feare thou work'st treason against my crown."

"My liege," quo' the abbot, "I would it were knowne,
I never spend nothing but what is my owne;
And I trust your grace will do me no deere,*
For spending of my own true-gotten Geere."

"Yes, yes, father abbot, thy fault it is highe,
And now for the same thou needest must dye;
For except thou canst answer me questions three,
Thy head shall be smitten from thy bodie."

"And first," quo' the king, "when I'm in this stead,
With my crowne of golde so faire on my head,
Among all my liege-men so noble of birth,
Thou must tell me to one penny what I am worthe."

"Secondlye, tell me, without any doubt,
How soon may I ride the whole world about.
And at the third question thou must not shrink,
But tell me here truly what I do think."

"O, these are hard questions for my shallow witt,
Nor I cannot answer your grace as yet:

* Deere: hurt

But if you will give me but three weeks' space,
I'le do my endeavour to answer your grace."

"Now three days' space to thee will I give,
And that is the longest time thou hast to live;
For if thou dost not answer my questions three,
Thy lands and thy livings are forfeit to me."

Away rode the abbot all sad at that word,
And he rode to Cambridge and Oxenford;
But never a doctor there was so wise,
That could with his learning an answer devise.

Then home rode the abbot of comfort so cold,
And he mett his shepherd a going to fold:
"How now, my lord abbot, you are welcome home:
What newes do you bring us from good King John?"

"Sad newes, sad newes, shepherd, I must give;
That I have but three days to live:
For if I do not answer him questions three,
My head will be smitten from my bodie."

"The first is to tell him there in that stead,
With his crowne of golde so fair on his head,
Among all his liege-men so noble of birth,
To within one penny of what he is worth."

"The seconde, to tell him, without any doubt,
How soone he may ride this whole world about;
And at the third question I must not shrinke,
But tell him there truly what he does thinke."

"Now cheare up, sire abbot; did you never hear yet,
That a foole he may learn a wise man witt?
Lend me your horse, and serving men, and your apparel,
And I'll ride to London to answer your quarrel."

>>

"Nay, frowne not, if it hath bin told unto me,
I am like your lordship as ever maybee:
And if you will but lend me your gowne,
There is none shall knowe us at fair London towne."

"Now horses and serving-men thou shalt have,
With sumptuous array most gallant and brave,
With crozier, and miter, and rochet, and cope,
Fit to appear 'fore our father the pope."

"Now welcome, sire abbot," the king he did say,
"Tis well thou'rt come back to keep thy day;
For and if thou canst answer my questions three,
Thy life and thy living both saved shall bee."

"And first when thou seest me here in this stead,
With my crown of golde so fair on my head,
Among all my liege-men so noble of birthe,
Tell me to one penny what I am worth."

"For thirty pence our Saviour was sold
Among the false Jews, as I have been told;
And twenty-nine is the worth of thee,
For I thinke thou art one penny worser than he."

The king he laughed, and swore by Saint Bittel,*
"I did not think I had been worth so littel!
— Now secondly, tell me, without any doubt,
How soone I may ride this whole world about."

"You must rise with the sun, and ride with the same,
Until the next morning he riseth againe;
And then your grace need not make any doubt,
But in twenty-four hours you'll ride it about."

The king he laughed, and swore by Saint Jone,
"I did not think it could be gone so soone!

* Meaning probably St Bottolph

— Now from the third question thou must not shrinke,
But tell me here truly what do I thinke."

"Yea, that I shall do, and make your grace merry:
You think I'm the Abbot of Canterbury;
But I'm his poor shepherd, as plain you may see,
That am come to beg pardon for him and for me."

The king he laughed, and swore by the masse,
"I'le make thee Lord Abbot this day in his place!"
"Nowe, naye, my liege, be not in such speede,
For, alacke, I can neither write nor reade."

"Four nobles a weeke then I will give thee,
For this merry jest thou hast showne unto me;
And tell the old abbot, when thou comst home,
Thou hast brought him a pardon from good King John."

The Charge of the Light Brigade

ALFRED, LORD TENNYSON

Half a league, half a league,
 Half a league onward,
All in the valley of Death
 Rode the six hundred.
"Forward the Light Brigade!
Charge for the guns!" he said:
Into the valley of Death
 Rode the six hundred.

"Forward the Light Brigade!"
Was there a man dismayed?
Not though the soldier knew
 Some one had blundered:
Their's not to make reply,
Their's not to reason why,
Their's but to do and die:
Into the valley of Death
 Rode the six hundred.

>>

Cannon to right of them,
Cannon to left of them,
Cannon in front of them
　　Volleyed and thundered;
Stormed at with shot and shell,
Boldly they rode and well,
Into the jaws of Death,
Into the mouth of Hell
　　Rode the six hundred.

Flashed all their sabres bare,
Flashed as they turned in air
Sabring the gunners there,
Charging an army, while
　　All the world wondered:
Plunged in the battery-smoke
Right through the line they broke;
Cossack and Russian
Reeled from the sabre-stroke
　　Shattered and sundered.
Then they rode back, but not,
　　Not the six hundred.

Cannon to right of them,
Cannon to left of them,
Cannon behind them
　　Volleyed and thundered;
Stormed at with shot and shell,
While horse and hero fell,
They that had fought so well
Came through the jaws of Death,
Back from the mouth of Hell,
All that was left of them,
　　Left of six hundred.

When can their glory fade?
O the wild charge they made!
　　All the world wondered.
Honour the charge they made!
Honour the Light Brigade,
　　Noble six hundred!

Kings and Queens

TRADITIONAL

First William the Norman,
    Then William his son;
Henry, Stephen, and Henry,
    Then Richard and John;
Next Henry the third,
    Edwards, one, two, and three,
And again after Richard
    Three Henrys we see.
Two Edwards, third Richard,
    If rightly I guess;
Two Henrys, sixth Edward,
    Queen Mary, Queen Bess.
Then Jamie the Scotchman,
    Then Charles, whom they slew,
Yet received after Cromwell
    Another Charles too.
Next James the second
    Ascended the throne;
Then good William and Mary
    Together came on.
Till Anne, Georges four
    And fourth William all past,
Came the reign of Victoria
    Which longest did last.
Then Edward the Peacemaker,
    He was her son,
And the fifth of the Georges
    Was next in the run;
Edward the Eighth
    Gave the crown to his brother,
Now God's sent Elizabeth:
    All of us love her.

Four Dates

TRADITIONAL

William the Conqueror, ten sixty-six,
Played on the Saxons oft-cruel tricks.

Columbus sailed the ocean blue,
In fourteen hundred and ninety-two.

The Spanish Armada met its fate,
In fifteen hundred and eighty-eight.

In sixteen hundred and sixty-six,
London burnt like rotten sticks.

Imagination

Eeka, Neeka

WALTER DE LA MARE

Eeka, Neeka, Leeka, Lee —
Here's a lock without a key;
Bring a lantern, bring a candle,
Here's a door without a handle;
Shine, shine, you old thief Moon,
Here's a door without a room;
Not a whisper, moth or mouse,
Key – lock – door – room: where's the house?

Say nothing, creep away,
And live to knock another day!

Tired Tim

WALTER DE LA MARE

Poor tired Tim! It's sad for him.
He lags the long bright morning through,
Ever so tired of nothing to do;
He moons and mopes the livelong day,
Nothing to think about, nothing to say;
Up to bed with his candle to creep,
Too tired to yawn, too tired to sleep:
Poor tired Tim! It's sad for him.

Some One

WALTER DE LA MARE

Some one came knocking
At my wee, small door;
Some one came knocking,
I'm sure — sure — sure;
I listened, I opened,
I looked to left and right,
But nought there was a-stirring
In the still dark night;
Only the busy beetle
Tap-tapping in the wall,
Only from the forest
The screech-owl's call,
Only the cricket whistling
While the dewdrops fall,
So I know not who came knocking
At all, at all, at all.

Silver

WALTER DE LA MARE

Slowly, silently, now the moon
Walks the night in her silver shoon;
This way, and that, she peers, and sees
Silver fruit upon silver trees;
One by one the casements catch
Her beams beneath the silvery thatch;
Couched in his kennel, like a log,
With paws of silver sleeps the dog;
From their shadowy cote the white breasts peep
Of doves in a silver-feathered sleep;
A harvest mouse goes scampering by,
With silver claws, and silver eye;
And moveless fish in the water gleam,
By silver reeds in a silver stream.

Martha

WALTER DE LA MARE

"Once ... once upon a time ..."
Over and over again,
Martha would tell us her stories,
In the hazel glen.

Hers were those clear grey eyes
You watch, and the story seems
Told by their beautifulness
Tranquil as dreams.

She'd sit with her two slim hands
Clasped round her bended knees;
While we on our elbows lolled,
And stared at ease.

Her voice and her narrow chin,
Her grave small lovely head,
Seemed half the meaning
Of the words she said.

"Once ... once upon a time ..."
Like a dream you dream in the night,
Fairies and gnomes stole out
In the leaf-green light.

And her beauty far away
Would fade, as her voice ran on,
Till hazel and summer sun
And all were gone:

All fordone and forgot;
And like clouds in the height of the sky,
Our hearts stood still in the hush
Of an age gone by.

Then

WALTER DE LA MARE

Twenty, forty, sixty, eighty,
    A hundred years ago,
All through the night with lantern bright
    The Watch trudged to and fro.
And little boys tucked snug abed
    Would wake from dreams to hear —
"Two o' the morning by the clock,
    And the stars a-shining clear!"
Or, when across the chimney tops
    Screamed shrill a North-East gale,
A faint and shaken voice would shout,
    "Three! — and a storm of hail!"

Over the Sea to Skye

ROBERT LOUIS STEVENSON

Sing me a song of a lad that is gone,
Say, could that lad be I?
Merry of soul he sailed on a day
Over the sea to Skye.

Mull was astern, Rum on the port,
Eigg on the starboard bow;
Glory of youth glowed in his soul:
Where is that glory now?

Sing me a song of a lad that is gone,
Say, could that lad be I?
Merry of soul he sailed on a day
Over the sea to Skye.

Billow and breeze, islands and seas,
Mountains of rain and sun,
All that was good, all that was fair,
All that was me is gone.

Old Meg

JOHN KEATS

Old Meg she was a gipsy,
And lived upon the moors;
Her bed it was the brown heath turf,
And her house was out of doors.

Her apples were swart blackberries,
Her currants, pods o' broom,
Her wine was dew o' the wild white rose,
Her book a churchyard tomb.

Her brothers were the craggy hills,
Her sisters larchen trees —
Alone with her great family
She lived as she did please.

No breakfast had she many a morn,
No dinner many a noon,
And 'stead of supper she would stare
Full hard against the moon.

But every morn of woodbine fresh
She made her garlanding,
And every night the dark glen yew
She wove, and she would sing.

And with her fingers, old and brown
She plaited mats o' rushes,
And gave them to the cottagers
She met among the bushes.

Old Meg was brave as Margaret Queen
And tall as Amazon,
An old red blanket cloak she wore;
A chip hat had she on.
God rest her agèd bones somewhere —
She died full long agone!

Time, you Old Gipsy Man

RALPH HODGSON

Time you old gipsy man
Will you not stay,
Put up your caravan
Just for one day?

All things I'll give you
Will you be my guest,
Bells for your jennet
Of silver the best,
Goldsmiths shall beat you
A great golden ring,
Peacocks shall bow to you,
Little boys sing,
Oh, and sweet girls will
Festoon you with may,
Time, you old gipsy,
Why hasten away?

Last week in Babylon,
Last night in Rome,
Morning, and in the crush
Under Paul's dome;
Under Paul's dial
You tighten your rein —
Only a moment,
And off once again;
Off to some city
Now blind in the womb,
Off to another
Ere that's in the tomb.

Time you old gipsy man,
Will you not stay,
Put up your caravan
Just for one day?

The Sailor's Consolation

WILLIAM PITT

One night came on a hurricane.
The sea was mountains rolling,
When Barney Buntline turned his quid
And said to Billy Bowling,
"A strong nor'-wester's blowing, Bill;
Hark! don't ye hear it roar now?
Lord help 'em, how I pities them
Unhappy folks on shore now!

"Fool-hardy chaps who live in towns,
What danger they are all in,
And now lie quaking in their beds,
For fear the roof should fall in:
Poor creatures, how they envies us,
And wishes, I've a notion,
For our good luck, in such a storm
To be upon the ocean.

"But as for them who're out all day,
On business, from their houses,
And late at night returning home
To cheer their babes and spouses;
While you and I, Bill, on the deck
Are comfortably lying,
My eyes! What tiles and chimney-pots
About their heads are flying!

"And very often we have heard
How men are killed and undone
By overturns from carriages,
By thieves and fires of London.
We know what risks all landsmen run,
From noblemen to tailors;
Then, Bill, let us thank Providence
That you and I are sailors!'

Cargoes

JOHN MASEFIELD

Quinquireme of Nineveh from distant Ophir
Rowing home to haven in sunny Palestine,
  With a cargo of ivory,
  And apes and peacocks,
Sandalwood, cedarwood, and sweet white wine.

Stately Spanish galleon coming from the Isthmus,
Dipping through the Tropics by the palm-green shores,
  With a cargo of diamonds,
  Emeralds, amethysts,
Topazes, and cinnamon, and gold moidores.

Dirty British coaster with a salt-caked smoke stack
Butting through the Channel in the mad March days,
  With a cargo of Tyne coal,
  Road-rail, Pig-lead,
Firewood, iron-ware, and cheap tin trays.

Puck's Song

RUDYARD KIPLING

See you the ferny ride that steals
Into the oak-woods far?
O that was whence they heaved the keels
That rolled to Trafalgar.

And mark you where the ivy clings
To Bayham's mouldering walls?
O there we cast the stout railings
That stand around Saint Paul's.

See you the dimpled track that runs,
All hollow through the wheat?
O that was where they hauled the guns
That smote King Philip's fleet!

Out of the Weald, the secret Weald,
Men sent in ancient years
The horse-shoes red at Flodden Field,
The arrows at Poitiers!

See you our little mill that clacks,
So busy by the brook?
She has ground her corn and paid her tax
Ever since Domesday Book.

See you our stilly woods of oak,
And the dread ditch beside?
O that was where the Saxons broke,
On the day that Harold died!

See you the windy levels spread
About the gates of Rye?
O that was where the Northmen fled,
When Alfred's ships came by!

See you our pastures wide and lone,
Where the red oxen browse?
O there was a City thronged and known,
Ere London boasted a house!

And see you, after rain, the trace
Of mound and ditch and wall?
O that was a Legion's camping-place,
When Caesar sailed from Gaul!

And see you the marks that show and fade,
Like shadows on the Downs?
O they are the lines the Flint men made,
To guard their wondrous towns!

Trackway and Camp and City lost,
Salt marsh where now is corn,
Old Wars, Peace, old Arts that cease,
And so was England born!

She is not any common Earth,
Water or Wood or Air,
But Merlin's Isle of Gramarye
Where you and I will fare.

The Lords of Shadow

FIONA MACLEOD

Where the water whispers 'mid the shadowy rowan-trees
I have heard the Hidden People like the hum of swarming bees:
And when the moon has risen and the brown burn glisters grey
I have seen the Green Host marching in laughing disarray.

Dalua then must sure have blown a sudden magic air
Or with the mystic dew have sealed my eyes from seeing fair:
For the great Lords of Shadow who tread the deeps of night
Are no frail puny folk who move in dread of mortal sight.

For sure Dalua laughed alow, Dalua the fairy Fool,
When with his wildfire eyes he saw me 'neath the rowan-shadowed pool:
His touch can make the chords of life a bitter jangling tune,
The false glows true, the true glows false, beneath his moontide rune.

The laughter of the Hidden Host is terrible to hear,
The Hounds of Death would harry me at lifting of a spear:
Mayhap Dalua made for me the hum of swarming bees
And sealed my eyes with dew beneath the shadowy rowan-trees.

Murias

FIONA MACLEOD

In the sunken city of Murias
    A golden Image dwells:
The sea-song of the trampling waves
    Is as muffled bells
    Where He dwells,
In the city of Murias.

In the sunken city of Murias
    A golden Image gleams:
The loud noise of the moving seas
    Is as woven beams
    Where He dreams,
In the city of Murias.

In the sunken city of Murias,
    Deep, deep beneath the sea
The Image sits and hears Time break
    The heart I gave to thee
    And thou to me,
In the city of Murias.

In the city of Murias,
    Long, oh, so long ago,
Our souls were wed when the world
    was young;
Are we old now, that we know
    This silent woe
In the city of Murias?

In the sunken city of Murias
    A graven Image dwells:
The sound of our little sobbing prayer
    Is as muffled bells
    Where He dwells,
In the city of Murias.

The Secret Gate

FIONA MACLEOD

From out the dark of sleep I rose, on the wings of desire:
"Give me the joy of sight," I cried, "O Master of Hidden Fire!"
    And a Voice said: *Wait*
    Till you pass the Gate.

"Give me the joy of sight," I cried, "O Master of Hidden Fire!
By the flame in the heart of the soul, grant my desire!"
    And a Voice said: *Wait*
    Till you pass the Gate.

I shook the dark with the tremulous beat of my wings of desire:
"Give me but once the thing I ask, O Master of Hidden Fire!"
    And a Voice said: *Wait!*
    You have reached the Gate.

I rose from flame to flame on pinions of desire:
And I heard the Voice of the Master of Hidden Fire:
    Behold the Flaming Gate
    Where Sight doth wait!

Like a wandering star I fell through the deeps of desire,
And back through the portals of sleep the Master of Hidden Fire
    Thundered: *Await*
    The opening of the Gate!

But now I pray, now I pray, with passionate desire:
"Blind me, O blind me, Master of Hidden Fire,
    I supplicate,
    Ope not the Gate."

The Arrow and the Song

HENRY WADSWORTH LONGFELLOW

I shot an arrow into the air,
It fell to earth, I knew not where;
For, so swiftly it flew, the sight
Could not follow it in its flight.

I breathed a song into the air,
It fell to earth, I knew not where;
For who has sight so keen and strong
That it can follow the flight of song?

Long, long afterward, in an oak
I found the arrow, still unbroke;
And the song, from beginning to end,
I found again in the heart of a friend.

The Splendour Falls on Castle Walls

From *The Princess*

Alfred, Lord Tennyson

The splendour falls on castle walls
And snowy summits old in story:
The long light shakes across the lakes,
And the wild cataract leaps in glory.
Blow, bugle, blow, set the wild echoes flying,
Blow, bugle; answer, echoes, dying, dying, dying.

O hark, O hear! how thin and clear,
And thinner, clearer, farther going!
O sweet and far from cliff and scar
The horns of Elfland faintly blowing!
Blow, let us hear the purple glens replying:
Blow, bugle; answer, echoes, dying, dying, dying.

O love, they die in yon rich sky,
They faint on hill or field or river:
Our echoes roll from soul to soul,
And grow for ever and for ever.
Blow, bugle, blow, set the wild echoes flying,
And answer, echoes, answer, dying, dying, dying.

Ode

A.W.E. O'SHAUGHNESSY

We are the music makers,
    And we are the dreamers of dreams,
Wandering by lone sea breakers,
    And sitting by desolate streams;
World-losers and world-forsakers,
    On whom the pale moon gleams:
Yet we are the movers and shakers
    Of the World for ever, it seems.

With wonderful deathless ditties
    We build up the world's great cities,
And out of a fabulous story
    We fashion an empire's glory:
One man with a dream, at pleasure,
    Shall go forth and conquer a crown;
And three with a new song's measure
    Can trample an empire down.

We, in the ages lying
    In the buried past of the earth,
Built Nineveh with our sighing,
    And Babel itself in our mirth;
And o'erthrew them prophesying
    To the Old of the New World's worth;
For each age is a dream that is dying,
    Or one that is coming to birth.

A breath of our inspiration
    Is the life of each generation;
A wondrous thing of our dreaming
    Unearthly, impossible seeming —
The soldier, the king and the peasant
    Are working together in one,
Till our dream shall become their present,
    And their work in the world be done.

They had no vision amazing
    Of the goodly house they are raising;

They had no divine foreshowing
 Of the land to which they are going:
But on one man's soul it hath broken,
 A light that doth not depart;
And his look, or a word he has spoken,
 Wrought flame in another man's heart.

And therefore today is thrilling
 With a past day's late fulfilling;
And the multitudes are enlisted
 In the faith that their fathers resisted,
And, scorning the dream of tomorrow,
 Are bringing to pass, as they may,
In the world, for its joy or its sorrow,
 The dream that was scorned yesterday.

But we, with our dreaming and singing,
 Ceaseless and Sorrowless we!
The glory about us clinging
 Of the glorious future we see
Our souls with high music ringing:
 O men! it must ever be
That we dwell in our dreaming and singing,
 A little apart from ye.

For we are afar with the dawning
 And the suns that are not yet high,
And out of the infinite morning
 Intrepid you hear us cry —
How, spite of your human scorning,
 Once more God's future draws nigh,
And already goes forth the warning
 That ye of the past must die.

Great hail! we cry to the comers
 From the dazzling unknown shore;
Bring us hither your sun and your summers,
 And renew our world as of yore;
You shall teach us your song's new numbers
 And things that we dreamed not before:
Yea, in spite of a dreamer who slumbers,
 And a singer who sings no more.

The Piper

WILLIAM BLAKE

Piping down the valleys wild,
Piping songs of pleasant glee,
On a cloud I saw a child,
And he laughing said to me:

"Pipe a song about a Lamb."
So I piped with merry chear.
"Piper, pipe that song again."
So I piped, he wept to hear.

"Drop thy pipe, thy happy pipe,
Sing thy songs of happy chear."
So I sung the same again
While he wept with joy to hear.

"Piper, sit thee down and write
In a book that all may read."
So he vanish'd from my sight.
And I pluck'd a hollow reed,

And I made a rural pen,
And I stain'd the water clear,
And I wrote my happy songs
Every child may joy to hear.

The Blind Boy

COLLEY CIBBER

O say what is that thing call'd Light
Which I must ne'er enjoy;
What are the blessings of the sight,
O tell your poor blind boy!

You talk of wondrous things you see,
You say the sun shines bright;
I feel him warm, but how can he
Or make it day or night?

My day or night myself I make
Whene'er I sleep or play;
And could I ever keep awake
With me 'twere always day.

With heavy sighs I often hear
You mourn my hapless woe;
Be sure with patience I can bear
A loss I ne'er can know.

Then let not what I cannot have
My cheer of mind destroy:
While thus I sing, I am a King,
Although a poor blind boy.

Night Mail

W.H. AUDEN

This is the Night Mail crossing the Border,
Bringing the cheque and the postal order,

Letters for the rich, letters for the poor,
The shop at the corner, the girl next door.

Pulling up Beattock, a steady climb:
The gradient's against her, but she's on time.

Past cotton-grass and moorland boulder,
Shovelling white steam over her shoulder,

Snorting noisily, she passes
Silent miles of wind-bent grasses. >>

Birds turn their heads as she approaches,
Stare from bushes at her blank-faced coaches.

Sheep-dogs cannot turn her course;
They slumber on with paws across.

In the farm she passes no one wakes,
But a jug in a bedroom gently shakes.

Dawn freshens. Her climb is done.
Down towards Glasgow she descends,
Towards the steam tugs yelping down the glade of cranes,
Towards the fields of apparatus, the furnaces
Set on the dark plain like gigantic chessmen.
All Scotland waits for her:
In dark glens, beside pale-green sea lochs,
Men long for news.

Letters of thanks, letters from banks,
Letters of joy from girl and boy,
Receipted bills and invitations
To inspect new stock or to visit relations,
And applications for situations,
And timid lovers' declarations,
And gossip, gossip from all the nations,
News circumstantial, news financial,
Letters with holiday snaps to enlarge in,
Letters with faces scrawled on the margin,
Letters from uncles, cousins and aunts,
Letters to Scotland from the South of France,
Letters of condolence to Highlands and Lowlands,
Written on paper of every hue,
The pink, the violet, the white and the blue,
The chatty, the catty, the boring, the adoring,
The cold and official and the heart's outpouring,
Clever, stupid, short and long,
The typed and the printed and the spelt all wrong.

Thousands are still asleep,
Dreaming of terrifying monsters
Or a friendly tea beside the band at Cranston's or Crawford's:
Asleep in working Glasgow, asleep in well-set Edinburgh,
Asleep in granite Aberdeen,
They continue their dreams,
But shall wake soon and hope for letters,
And none will hear the postman's knock
Without a quickening of the heart.
For who can bear to feel himself forgotten?

A Tale of Acadie

From *Evangeline*

HENRY WADSWORTH LONGFELLOW

This is the forest primeval. The murmuring pines and the hemlocks,
Bearded with moss, and in garments green, indistinct in the twilight,
Stand like Druids of eld, with voices sad and prophetic,
Stand like harpers hoar, with beards that rest on their bosoms.
Loud from its rocky caverns, the deep-voiced neighbouring ocean
Speaks, and in accents disconsolate answers the wail of the forest.

This is the forest primeval; but where are the hearts that beneath it
Leaped like the roe, when he hears in the woodland the voice of the huntsman?
Where is the thatch-roofed village, the home of Acadian farmers,
Men whose lives glided on like rivers that water the woodlands,
Darkened by shadows of earth, but reflecting an image of heaven?
Waste are those pleasant farms, and the farmers forever departed!
Scattered like dust and leaves, when the mighty blasts of October
Seize them and whirl them aloft, and sprinkle them far o'er the ocean;
Naught but tradition remains of the beautiful village of Grand-Pré.

Ye who believe in affection that hopes, and endures, and is patient,
Ye who believe in the beauty and strength of woman's devotion,
List to the mournful tradition still sung by the pines of the forest;
List to a Tale of Love in Acadie, home of the happy.

Welsh Incident

ROBERT GRAVES

"But that was nothing to what things came out
From the sea caves of Criccieth yonder."
"What were they? Mermaids? dragons? ghosts?"
"Nothing at all of any things like that."
"What were they, then?"

"All sorts of queer things,
Things never seen or heard or written about,
Very strange, un-Welsh, utterly peculiar
Things. Oh, solid enough they seemed to touch,
Had anyone dared it. Marvellous creation,
All various shapes and sizes, and no sizes,
All new, each perfectly unlike his neighbour,
Though all came moving slowly out together."
"Describe just one of them."

"I am unable."
"What were their colours?"
"Mostly nameless colours,
Colours you'd like to see; but one was puce
Or perhaps more like crimson, but not purplish.
Some had no colour."
"Tell me had they legs?"
"Not a leg nor foot among them that I saw."
"But did these things come out in any order?
What o'clock was it? What was the day of the week?
Who else was present? How was the weather?"
"I was coming to that. It was half-past three
On Easter Tuesday last. The sun was shining.
The Harlech Silver Band played *Marchog Jesu*
On thirty-seven shimmering instruments,
Collecting for Caernarvon's (Fever) Hospital Fund.
The populations of Pwllheli, Criccieth,
Portmadoc, Borth, Tremadoc, Penrhyndeudraeth,
Were all assembled. Criccieth's Mayor addressed them
First in good Welsh and then in fluent English,

Twisting his fingers in his chain of office,
Welcoming the things. They came out on the sand,
Not keeping time to the band, moving seaward
Silently at a snail's pace. But at last
The most odd, indescribable thing of all,
Which hardly one man there could see for wonder,
Did something recognizably a something."
"Well, what?"
"It made a noise."
"A frightening noise?"
"No, no."
"A musical noise? A noise of scuffling?"
"No, but a very loud, respectable noise —
Like groaning to oneself on Sunday morning
In Chapel, close before the second psalm."
"What did the Mayor do?"
"I was coming to that."

The Chambered Nautilus

OLIVER WENDELL HOLMES

This is the ship of pearl, which, poets feign,
Sails the unshadowed main —
The venturous bark that flings
On the sweet summer wind its purpled wings
In gulfs enchanted, where the siren sings,
And the coral reefs lie bare,
Where the cold sea-maids rise to sun their streaming hair.

Its web of living gauze no more unfurl,
Wrecked is the ship of pearl!
And every chambered cell,
Where its dim dreaming life was wont to dwell
As the frail tenant shaped his growing shell,
Before thee lies revealed —
Its irised ceiling rent, its sunless crypt unsealed!

>>

Year after year beheld the silent toil,
    That spread his lustrous coil.
Still, as the spiral grew,
    He left the past year's dwelling for the new
Stole with soft step its shining archway through,
    Built up its idle door,
Stretched in his last-found home, and knew the old no more.

Thanks for the heavenly message brought by thee,
    Child of the wandering sea,
Cast from her lap, forlorn!
    From thy dead lips a clearer note is born,
Than ever Triton blew from wreathed horn,
    While on mine ear it rings,
Through the deep caves of thought I hear a voice that sings.

Build thee more stately mansions, O my soul,
    As the swift seasons roll!
Leave thy low-vaulted past!
    Let each new temple, nobler than the last,
Shut thee from heaven with a dome more vast,
    Till thou at length art free,
Leaving thine outgrown shell by life's unresting sea.

– – – ❖ – – – –

Shakespeare

– – – ❖ – – – –

Puck's Song

FROM *A MIDSUMMER NIGHT'S DREAM*

Over hill, over dale,
    Thorough bush, thorough brier,
Over park, over pale,
    Thorough flood, thorough fire,
I do wander everywhere,
Swifter than the moon's sphere;
And I serve the Fairy Queen,
To dew her orbs upon the green.
The cowslips tall her pensioners be;
In their gold coats spots you see;
Those be rubies, fairy favours,
In those freckles live their savours.
I must go seek some dewdrops here,
And hang a pearl in every cowslip's ear.

The Merry Heart

Jog on, jog on, the footpath way,
And merrily hent the stile-a;
A merry heart goes all the day,
Your sad tires in a mile-a.

Ariel's Dirge

FROM *THE TEMPEST*

Full fathom five thy father lies;
Of his bones are coral made;
Those are pearls that were his eyes:
Nothing of him that doth fade,
But doth suffer a sea-change
Into something rich and strange.
Sea-nymphs hourly ring his knell:
Ding-dong.
Hark! now I hear them — ding-dong, bell.

The Witches' Spell

FROM *MACBETH*

FIRST WITCH: Thrice the brinded* cat hath mew'd.

SECOND WITCH: Thrice and once the hedge-pig whin'd.

THIRD WITCH: Harpier† cries: 'Tis time, 'tis time.

FIRST WITCH: Round about the cauldron go;
In the poison'd entrails throw.
Toad that under cold stone
Days and nights has thirty-one
Swelter'd venom sleeping got
Boil thou first i' the charmed pot.

ALL: Double, double toil and trouble;
Fire burn, and cauldron bubble.

* brinded: tabby

† Harpier: familiar spirit, or demon under her power; harpy; a fabulous creature with a woman's body and bird's wings and claws

SECOND WITCH: Fillet of a fenny* snake,
In the cauldron boil and bake;
Eye of newt, and toe of frog,
Wool of bat, and tongue of dog,
Adder's fork, and blind-worm's sting,
Lizard's leg, and howlet's wing,
For a charm of powerful trouble,
Like a hell-broth boil and bubble.

ALL: Double, double toil and trouble;
Fire burn, and cauldron bubble.

THIRD WITCH: Scale of dragon, tooth of wolf,
Witches' mummy, maw and gulf
Of the ravin'd salt-sea shark,
Root of hemlock digg'd i' the dark,
Liver of blaspheming Jew,
Gall of goat, and slips of yew
Sliver'd in the moon's eclipse,
Nose of Turk, and Tartar's lips,
Finger of birth-strangled babe
Ditch-deliver'd by a drab,
Make the gruel thick and slab:
Add thereto a tiger's chaudron,†
For the ingredients of our cauldron.

ALL: Double, double toil and trouble;
Fire burn, and cauldron bubble.

SECOND WITCH: Cool it with a baboon's blood,
Then the charm is firm and good.

* fenny: from a fen or swamp
† chaudron: entrails

Sonnet LXV

Since brass, nor stone, nor earth, nor boundless sea,
But sad mortality o'ersways their power,
How with this rage shall beauty hold a plea,
Whose action is no stronger than a flower?
O how shall summer's honey breath hold out
Against the wreckful siege of battering days,
When rocks impregnable are not so stout,
Nor gates of steel so strong, but Time decays?
O fearful meditation! Where, alack!
Shall Time's best jewel from Time's chest lie hid?
Or what strong hand can hold his swift foot back?
Or who his spoil of beauty can forbid?
    O none, unless this miracle have might,
    That in black ink my love may still shine bright.

Sonnet CXLVI

Poor Soul, the centre of my sinful earth,
Fool'd by these rebel powers that thee array,
Why dost thou pine within, and suffer dearth,
Painting thy outward walls so costly gay?
Why so large cost, having so short a lease,
Dost thou upon thy fading mansion spend?
Shall worms, inheritors of this excess,
Eat up thy charge? Is this thy body's end?
Then, soul, live thou upon thy servant's loss,
And let that pine to aggravate thy store;
Buy terms divine in selling hours of dross;
Within be fed, without be rich no more:
    So shalt thou feed on Death, that feeds on men,
    And Death once dead, there's no more dying then.

– – – ❖ – – –

Narrative Poems

– – – ❖ – – –

From *The Pied Piper of Hamelin*

ROBERT BROWNING

Hamelin Town's in Brunswick,
By famous Hanover city;
The river Weser, deep and wide,
Washes its wall on the southern side;

A pleasanter spot you never spied;
But, when begins my ditty,
Almost five hundred years ago,
To see the townsfolk suffer so
From vermin, was a pity.

Rats!
They fought the dogs and killed the cats,
And bit the babies in the cradles,
And ate the cheeses out of the vats,
And licked the soup from the cooks' own ladles,
Split open the kegs of salted sprats,
Made nests inside men's Sunday hats,
And even spoiled the women's chats
By drowning their speaking
With shrieking and squeaking
In fifty different sharps and flats.

>>

At last the people in a body
To the Town Hall came flocking:
"Tis clear," cried they, "our Mayor's a noddy;
And as for our Corporation — shocking
To think we buy gowns lined with ermine
For dolts that can't or won't determine
What's best to rid us of our vermin!
You hope, because you're old and obese,
To find in the furry civic robe ease?
Rouse up, sirs! Give your brains a racking
To find the remedy we're lacking,
Or, sure as fate, we'll send you packing!"
At this the Mayor and Corporation
Quaked with a mighty consternation.

An hour they sat in council,
At length the Mayor broke silence:
"For a guilder I'd my ermine gown sell,
I wish I were a mile hence!
It's easy to bid one rack one's brain —
I'm sure my poor head aches again,
I've scratched it so, and all in vain.
Oh for a trap, a trap, a trap!"
Just as he said this, what should hap
At the chamber door but a gentle tap? ...

"Come in!" — the Mayor cried, looking bigger:
And in did come the strangest figure!
His queer long coat from heel to head
Was half of yellow and half of red,
And he himself was tall and thin,
With sharp blue eyes, each like a pin,
And light loose hair, yet swarthy skin,
No tuft on cheek nor beard on chin,
But lips where smiles went out and in;
There was no guessing his kith and kin:
And nobody could enough admire
The tall man and his quaint attire ...

He advanced to the council-table:
And, "Please your honours," said he, "I'm able,
By means of a secret charm, to draw
    All creatures living beneath the sun,
    That creep or swim or fly or run,
After me so as you never saw!
And I chiefly use my charm
On creatures that do people harm,
The mole and toad and newt and viper;
And people call me the Pied Piper." ...

"And as for what your brain bewilders,
    If I can rid your town of rats
Will you give me a thousand guilders?"
"One? Fifty thousand!" — was the exclamation
Of the astonished Mayor and Corporation.

Into the street the Piper stept,
    Smiling first a little smile,
As if he knew what magic slept
    In his quiet pipe the while;
Then, like a musical adept,
To blow the pipe his lips he wrinkled,
And green and blue his sharp eyes twinkled,
Like a candle-flame where salt is sprinkled;
And ere three shrill notes the pipe uttered,
You heard as if an army muttered;
And the muttering grew to a grumbling;
And the grumbling grew to a mighty rumbling;
And out of the houses the rats came tumbling.
Great rats, small rats, lean rats, brawny rats,
Brown rats, black rats, grey rats, tawny rats,
Grave old plodders, gay young friskers,
    Fathers, mothers, uncles, cousins,
Cocking tails and pricking whiskers,
    Families by tens and dozens,
Brothers, sisters, husbands, wives —
Followed the Piper for their lives.
From street to street he piped advancing, >>

And step for step they followed dancing,
Until they came to the river Weser,
Wherein all plunged and perished! ...

You should have heard the Hamelin people
Ringing the bells till they rocked the steeple.
"Go," cried the Mayor, "and get long poles,
Poke out the nests and block up the holes!
Consult with carpenters and builders,
And leave in our town not even a trace
Of the rats!" — when suddenly, up the face
Of the Piper perked in the market-place,
With a "First, if you please, my thousand guilders!"

A thousand guilders! The Mayor looked blue;
And so did the Corporation too ...
To pay this sum to a wandering fellow
With a gipsy coat of red and yellow!
"Beside," quoth the Mayor with a knowing wink,
Our business was done at the river's brink;
We saw with our eyes the vermin sink,
And what's dead can't come to life, I think.
So, friend, we're not the folks to shrink
From the duty of giving you something for drink,
And a matter of money to put in your poke;
But as for the guilders, what we spoke
Of them, as you very well know, was in joke.
Beside, our losses have made us thrifty.
A thousand guilders! Come, take fifty!'

The Piper's face fell, and he cried
"No trifling! I can't wait, beside! ...
And folks who put me in a passion
May find me pipe after another fashion." ...

"You threaten us, fellow? Do your worst,
Blow your pipe there till you burst!"

Once more he stept in to the street
    And to his lips again
    Laid his long pipe of smooth straight cane;
And 'ere he blew three notes (such sweet
Soft notes as yet musician's cunning
    Never gave the enraptured air)
There was a rustling that seemed like a bustling
Of merry crowds justling at pitching and hustling,
Small feet were pattering, wooden shoes clattering,
And, like fowls in a farm-yard when barley
    is scattering,
Out came the children running.
All the little boys and girls,
With rosy cheeks and flaxen curls,
And sparkling eyes and teeth like pearls,
Tripping and skipping, ran merrily after
The wonderful music with shouting and laughter.

The Mayor was dumb, and the Council stood
As if they were changed into blocks of wood,
Unable to move a step, or cry
To the children merrily skipping by,
— Could only follow with the eye
That joyous crowd at the Piper's back.
But how the Mayor was on the rack,
And the wretched Council's bosoms beat,
As the Piper turned from the High Street
To where the Weser rolled its waters
Right in the way of their sons and daughters!
However he turned from South to West,
And to Koppelberg Hill his steps addressed,
And after him the children pressed;
Great was the joy in every breast.
"He never can cross that mighty top!
He's forced to let the piping drop,
And we shall see our children stop!"
When, lo, as they reached the mountainside,
A wondrous portal opened wide,
As if a cavern was suddenly hollowed; >>

And the Piper advanced and the children followed,
And when all were in to the very last,
The door in the mountain-side shut fast.
Did I say all? No! One was lame,
    And could not dance the whole of the way;
And in after years, if you would blame
His sadness, he was used to say, —
"It's dull in our town since my playmates left!
I can't forget that I'm bereft
Of all the pleasant sights they see,
Which the Piper also promised me.
For he led us, he said, to a joyous land,
Joining the town and just at hand,
Where waters gushed and fruit-trees grew
And flowers put forth a fairer hue,
And everything was strange and new;
The sparrows were brighter than peacocks here,
And their dogs outran our fallow deer,
And honey-bees had lost their stings,
And horses were born with eagles' wings:
And just as I became assured
My lame foot would be speedily cured,
The music stopped and I stood still,
And found myself outside the hill,
Left alone against my will,
To go now limping as before,
And never hear of that country more!" ...

The Mayor sent East, West, North and South,
To offer the Piper, by word of mouth,
    Wherever it was men's lot to find him,
Silver and gold to his heart's content,
If only he'd return the way he went,
    And bring the children behind him.
But when they saw 'twas a lost endeavour,
And Piper and dancers were gone for ever ...
    They wrote the story on a column,
And on the great church-window painted
The same, to make the world acquainted

How their children were stolen away,
And there it stands to this very day ...

So Willy, let me and you be wipers
Of scores out with all men — especially pipers!
And, whether they pipe us free from rats
    or from mice,
If we've promised them aught, let us keep
    our promise!

The Leap of Roushan Beg

HENRY WADSWORTH LONGFELLOW

Mounted on Kyrat strong and fleet,
His chestnut steed with four white feet,
    Roushan Beg, called Kurroglou,
Son of the road and bandit chief,
Seeking refuge and relief,
    Up the mountain pathway flew.

Such was Kyrat's wondrous speed,
Never yet could any steed
    Reach the dust-cloud in his course.
More than maiden, more than wife,
More than gold, and next to life
    Roushan the Robber loved his horse.

In the land that lies beyond
Erzeroum and Trebizond,
    Garden-girt his fortress stood;
Plundered khan, or caravan
Journeying north from Koordistan,
    Gave him wealth and wine and food.

Seven hundred and fourscore
Men-at-arms his livery wore,
    Did his bidding night and day, >>

Now, through regions all unknown,
He was wandering, lost, alone,
    Seeking without guide his way.

Suddenly the pathway ends,
Sheer the precipice descends,
    Loud the torrent roars unseen;
Thirty feet from side to side
Yawns the chasm; on air must ride
    He who crosses this ravine.

Following close in his pursuit,
At the precipice's foot,
    Reyhan the Arab of Orfah
Halted with his hundred men,
Shouting upward from the glen,
    "La Illah illa Allah."

Gently Roushan Beg caressed
Kyrat's forehead, neck, and breast,
    Kissed him upon both his eyes;
Sang to him in his wild way,
As upon the topmost spray
    Sings a bird before it flies.

"O my Kyrat, O my steed
Round and slender as a reed
    Carry me this peril through!
Satin housings shall be thine,
Shoes of gold, O Kyrat mine,
    O thou soul of Kurroglou!

Soft thy skin as silken skein,
Soft as woman's hair thy mane,
    Tender are thine eyes and true;
All thy hoofs like ivory shine,
Polished bright; O life of mine,
    Leap, and rescue Kurroglou!"

Kyrat, then, the strong and fleet,
Drew together his four white feet,
    Paused a moment on the verge,
Measured with his eye the space,
And into the air's embrace
    Leaped as leaps the ocean surge.

As the ocean surge o'er sand
Bears a swimmer safe to land,
    Kyrat safe his rider bore;
Rattling down the deep abyss
Fragments of the precipice
    Rolled like pebbles on a shore.

Roushan's tassled cap of red
Trembled not upon his head,
    Careless sat he and upright;
Neither hand nor bridle shook,
Nor his head he turned to look,
    As he galloped out of sight.

Flash of harness in the air,
Seen a moment like the glare
    Of a sword drawn from its sheath,
Thus the phantom horseman passed,
And the shadow that he cast
    Leaped the cataract underneath.

Reyhan the Arab held his breath
While this vision of life and death
    Passed above him "Allahu!"
Cried he. "In all Koordistan
Lives there not so brave a man
    As this Robber Kurroglou!"

From *The Peace-pipe*

Henry Wadsworth Longfellow

Gitche Manito, the mighty,
The creator of the nations,
Looked upon them with compassion,
With paternal love and pity;
Looked upon their wrath and wrangling
But as quarrels among children,
But as feuds and fights of children!

Over them he stretched his right hand,
To subdue their stubborn natures,
To allay their thirst and fever,
By the shadow of his right hand;
Spake to them with voice majestic,
As the sound of far-off waters
Falling into deep abysses,
Warning, chiding, spake in this wise —

"O my children! my poor children!
Listen to the words of wisdom,
Listen to the words of warning,
From the lips of the Great Spirit,
From the Master of Life, who made you!
I have given you lands to hunt in,
I have given you streams to fish in,
I have given you bear and bison,
I have given you roe and reindeer,
I have given you brant and beaver,
Filled the marshes full of wild-fowl,
Filled the rivers full of fishes;
Why then are you not contented?
Why then will you hunt each other?

I am weary of your quarrels,
Weary of your wars and bioodshed,
Weary of your prayers for vengeance,
Of your wranglings and dissensions;

All your strength is in your union,
All your danger is in discord;
Therefore be at peace hence forward,
And as brothers live together."

Yussouf

J.R. LOWELL

A stranger came one night to Yussouf's tent,
Saying — "Behold one outcast and in dread,
Against whose life the bow of Power is bent,
Who flies, and hath not where to lay his head.
I come to thee for shelter and for food:
To Yussouf, call'd through all our tribes the Good."

"This tent is mine," said Yussouf — "but no more
Than it is God's: come in and be at peace;
Freely shalt thou partake of all my store,
As I of His who buildeth over these
Our tents His glorious roof of night and day,
And at whose door none ever yet heard Nay."

So Yussouf entertained his guest that night;
And waking him ere day, said — "Here is gold;
My swiftest horse is saddled for thy flight,
Depart before the prying day grow bold!"
As one lamp lights another, nor grows less,
So nobleness enkindleth nobleness.

That inward light the stranger's face made grand
Which shines from all self-conquest; kneeling low,
He bow'd his forehead upon Yussouf's hand,
Sobbing — "O Sheikh! I cannot leave thee so —
I will repay thee — all this thou hast done
Unto that Ibrahim who slew thy son!"

>>

"Take the gold!" said Yussouf — "far with thee
Into the desert, never to return,
My one black thought shall ride away from me.
First-born, for whom by day and night I yearn,
Balanced and just are all of God's decrees;
Thou are avenged, my First-born! Sleep in peace."

Eddi's Service

RUDYARD KIPLING

Eddi, priest of Saint Wilfrid
In his chapel at Manhood End,
Ordered a midnight service
For such as cared to attend.

But the Saxons were keeping Christmas,
    And the night was stormy as well.
Nobody came to service,
    Though Eddi rang the bell.

"Wicked weather for walking,"
    Said Eddi of Manhood End.
"But I must go on with the service
    For such as care to attend."

The altar-lamps were lighted —
    An old marsh-donkey came,
Bold as a guest invited,
    And stared at the guttering flame.

The storm beat on at the windows,
    The water splashed on the floor
And a wet, yoke-weary bullock
    Pushed in through the open door.

"How do I know what is greatest
How do I know what is least?
That is my Father's business,"
Said Eddi, Wilfrid's priest.

"But three are gathered together —
    Listen to me and attend,
I bring good news, my brethren!"
    Said Eddi of Manhood End.

And he told the Ox of a Manger
    And a stall in Bethlehem,
And he spoke to the Ass of a Rider
    That rode to Jerusalem.

They steamed and dripped in the chancel,
    They listened and never stirred,
While, just as though they were Bishops,
    Eddi preached them the Word.

Till the gale blew off the marshes
    And the windows showed the day,
And the Ox and the Ass together
    Wheeled and clattered away.

When the Saxons mocked him
    Said Eddi of Manhood End,
"I dare not shut this chapel
    On such as care to attend."

The Ballad of Semmerwater

WILLIAM WATSON

Deep asleep, deep asleep
Deep asleep it lies,
The still lake of Semmerwater
Under the still skies.
And many a fathom, many a fathom,
Many a fathom below
In a king's tower and a queen's bower
The fishes come and go.

>>

Once there stood by Semmerwater
A mickle tower and tall
King's tower and queen's bower
And the wakeman on the wall.

Came a beggar halt and sore:
"I faint for lack of bread."
King's tower and queen's bower
Cast him forth unfed.
He knocked at the door of the eller
The eller's cot in the dale,
They gave him of their oat cake
They gave him of their ale.

He has cursed aloud that city
He has cursed it in his pride;
He has cursed it into Semmerwater
There to bide.
King's tower and queen's bower
And a mickle tower tall,
By glimmer of scale and gleam of fin
Folk have seen them all.
King's tower and queen's bower
And weed and reed in the gloom
And a lost city in Semmerwater
Deep asleep till doom.

The Elf Stroke

TRANSLATED FROM THE DANISH

Sir Olaf has ridden far and wide
The folk to his wedding feast to bid.

The elves, they dance in a fairy ring
And the elf king's daughter she beckons to him.

"Now welcome Sir Olaf, tarry a wee
Step into the ring and dance with me."

"I must not dance and I dare not stay,
Tomorrow it is my wedding day!"

"Light down, Sir Olaf, and dance with me
And two gold spurs I will give to thee:

A scarf too, of silk so white and fine
My mother bleached it in pale moonshine."

"I must not dance and I dare not stay,
Tomorrow it is my wedding day!"

"Light down, Sir Olaf, and dance with me,
And a heap of gold I'll give to thee."

"O well I like the golden glance,
But not for that with thee I'll dance."

"And if thou wilt not dance with me,
A bane and a blight shall follow thee!"

She struck him a blow right over the heart,
It chilled him through with a wondrous smart.

Pale grew his cheek as he turned to ride
"Now! Get thee home to thy winsome bride!"

And when to his castle door he sped
His mother stood waiting, all adread.

"Now tell to me, Sir Olaf, my son,
What makes thy cheek so pale and wan?"

"O well may it be wan and pale
I've seen the elf-folk in the vale!"

"Alas for thee my son, my pride
What shall I say to thy bonny bride?"

"Tell her that I'm to the forest bound
To prove my steed and my good grey hound."

Right early when the day had broke,
The bride she came with her bridal folk.

They dealt out meat and they dealt out wine;
"Now where is Sir Olaf, this groom of mine?" >>

"Sir Olaf is gone to the forest bound
To prove his steed and his good grey hound."

The bride she lifted the mantel-red;
There lay Sir Olaf ... and he was dead.

The Bridge-Keeper's Story

W.A. Eaton

"Do we have many accidents here, sir?"
"Well, no! but of one I could tell,
If you wouldn't mind hearing the story,
I have cause to remember it well!

You see how the drawbridge swings open
When the vessels come in from the bay,
When the New York express comes along, sir!
The bridge must be shut right away!

You see how it's worked by the windlass,
A child, sir, could manage it well,
My brave little chap used to do it,
But that's part of the tale I must tell!

It is two years ago come the autumn,
I shall never forget it, I'm sure;
I was sitting at work in the house here,
And the boy played just outside the door!

You must know, that the wages I'm getting
For the work on the line are not great,
So I picked up a little shoemaking,
And I managed to live at that rate.

I was pounding away on my lapstone,
And singing as blithe as could be!
Keeping time with the tap of my hammer
On the work that I held at my knee.

And Willie, my golden-haired darling,
Was tying a tail on his kite;
His cheeks all aglow with excitement,
And his blue eyes lit up with delight.

When the telegraph bell at the station
Rang out the express on its way;
'All right, father!' shouted my Willie,
'Remember, I'm pointsman today!'

I heard the wheel turn at the windlass,
I heard the bridge swing on its way,
And there came a cry from my darling,
A cry, filled my heart with dismay.

'Help, father! Oh help me!' he shouted.
I sprang through the door with a scream,
His clothes had got caught in the windlass,
There he hung o'er the swift, rushing stream.

And there, like a speck in the distance,
I saw the fleet oncoming train;
And the bridge that I thought safely fastened,
Unclosed and swung backward again.

I rushed to my boy, ere I reached him,
He fell in the river below.
I saw his bright curls on the water,
Borne away by the current's swift flow.

I sprang to the edge of the river,
But there was the onrushing train,
And hundreds of lives were in peril,
Till that bridge was refastened again.

I heard a loud shriek just behind me,
I turned, and his mother stood there,
Looking just like a statue of marble,
With her hands clasped in agonized prayer.

>>

Should I leap in the swift-flowing torrent
While the train went headlong to its fate,
Or stop to refasten the drawbridge,
And go to his rescue too late?

I looked at my wife and she whispered,
With choking sobs stopping her breath,
'Do your duty, and heaven will help you
To save our own darling from death!'

Quick as thought, then, I flew to the windlass,
And fastened the bridge with a crash,
Then just as the train rushed across it,
I leaped in the stream with a splash.

How I fought with the swift-rushing water,
How I battled till hope almost fled,
But just as I thought I had lost him,
Up floated his bright golden head.

How I eagerly seized on his girdle,
As a miser would clutch at his gold,
But the snap of his belt came unfastened,
And the swift stream unloosened my hold.

He sank once again, but I followed,
And caught at his bright clustering hair,
And biting my lip till the blood came,
I swam with the strength of despair!

We had got to a bend of the river,
Where the water leaps down with a dash,
I held my boy tighter than ever,
And steeled all my nerves for the crash.

The foaming and thundering whirlpool
Engulfed us, I struggled for breath,
Then caught on a crag in the current,
Just saved, for a moment, from death!

And there on the bank stood his mother,
And some sailors were flinging a rope,
It reached us at last, and I caught it,
For I knew 'twas our very last hope!

And right up the steep rock they dragged us,
I cannot forget, to this day,
How I clung to the rope, while my darling
In my arms like a dead baby lay.

And down in the greensward I laid him
Till the colour came back to his face,
And, oh, how my heart beat with rapture
As I felt his warm, loving embrace!

There sir, that's my story, a true one,
Though it's far more exciting than some,
It has taught me a lesson, and that is,
'Do your duty, whatever may come!'"

St Christopher of the Gael

FIONA MACLEOD

Behind the wattle-woven house
Nial the Mighty gently crept
From out a screen of ashtree boughs
To where a captive white-robe slept.

Lightly he moved, as though ashamed;
To right and left he glanced his fears.
Nial the Mighty was he named
Though but an untried youth in years —

But tall he was, as tall as he,
White Dermid of the magic sword,
Or Torcall of the Hebrid Sea,
Or great Cuhoolin of the Ford;

>>

Strong as the strongest, too, he was:
As Balor of the Evil Eye;
As Fionn who kept the Ulster Pass
From dawn till blood-flusht sunset sky.

Much had he pondered all that day
The mystery of the men who died
On crosses raised along the way,
And perished singing side by side.

Modred the chief had sailed the Moyle,
Had reached Iona's guardless-shore,
Had seized the monks when at their toil
And carried northward, bound, a score.

Some he had thrust into the deep,
To see if magic fins would rise:
Some from high rocks he forced to leap,
To see wings fall from out the skies:

Some he had pinned upon tall spears,
Some tossed on shields with brazen clang,
To see if through their blood and tears
Their god would hear the hymns they sang.

But when his oarsmen flung their oars,
And laughed to see across the foam
The glimmer of the highland shores
And smoke-wreaths of the hidden home,

Modred was weary of his sport.
All day he brooded as he strode
Betwixt the reef-encircled port
And the oak-grove of the Sacred Road.

At night he bade his warriors raise
Seven crosses where the foamswept strand
Lay still and white beyond the blaze
Of the hundred camp-fires of the land.

The women milked the late-come kye,
The children raced in laughing glee;
Like sheep from out the fold of the sky
Stars leapt and stared at earth and sea.

At times a wild and plaintive air
Made delicate music far away:
A hill-fox barked before its lair:
The white owl hawked its shadowy prey.

But at the rising of the moon
The druids came from grove and glen,
And to the chanting of a rune
Crucified Saint Columba's men.

They died in silence side by side,
But first they sang the evening hymn:
By midnight all but one had died,
At dawn he too was grey and grim.

One monk alone had Modred kept,
A youth with hair of golden-red
Who never once had sighed or wept,
Not once had bowed his proud young head.

Broken he lay, and bound with thongs.
Thus had he seen his brothers toss
Like crows transfixed upon great prongs,
Till death crept up each silent cross.

Night grew to dawn, to scarlet morn;
Day waned to firelit, starlit night:
But still with eyes of passionate scorn
He dared the worst of Modred's might.

When from the wattle-woven house
Nial the Mighty softly stepped,
And peered beneath the ashtree boughs
To where he thought the whiterobe slept,

>>

He heard the monk's word rise in prayer,
He heard a hymn's ascending breath —
Christ, Son of God, to Thee I fare
This night upon the wings of death.

Nial the Mighty crossed the space,
He waited till the monk had ceased;
Then, leaning o'er the foam-white face,
He stared upon the dauntless priest.

"Speak low," he said, "and tell me this:
'Who is the king you hold so great? —
Your eyes are dauntless flames of bliss
Though Modred taunts you with his hate —

This god or king, is He more strong
Than Modred is! And does He sleep
That thus your death-in-life is long,
And bonds your aching body keep?"

The monk's eyes stared in Nial's eyes:
"Young giant with a child's white heart,
I see a cross take shape and rise,
And thou upon it nailed art!"

Nial looked back: no cross he saw
Looming from out the dreadful night:
Yet all his soul was filled with awe,
A thundercloud with heart of light.

"Tell me thy name," he said, "and why
Thou waitest thus the druid knife,
And carest not to live or die?
Monk, hast thou little care of life?"

"Great care of that I have," he said,
And looked at Nial with eyes of fire:
"My life begins when I am dead,
There only is my heart's desire."

Nial the Mighty sighed. "Thy words
Are as the idle froth of foam,
Or clashing of triumphant swords
When Modred brings the foray home.

'My name is Nial: Nial the Strong:
A lad in years, but as you see
More great than heroes of old song
Or any lordly men that be.

To Modred have I come from far,
O'er many a hill and strath and stream,
To be a mighty sword in war,
And this because I dreamed a dream:

My dream was that my strength so great
Should serve the greatest king there is:
Modred the Pict thus all men rate,
And so I sought this far-off Liss.

But if there be a greater yet,
A king or god whom he doth fear,
My service he shall no more get,
My strength shall rust no longer here."

The monk's face gladdened. "Go, now, go;
To Modred go: he sitteth dumb,
And broods on what he fain would know:
And say, *O King, the Cross is come!*

Then shall the king arise in wrath,
And bid you go from out his sight,
For if he meet you on his path
He'll leave you stark and still and white.

Thus shall he show, great king and all,
He fears the glorious Cross of Christ,
And dreads to hear slain voices call
For vengeance on the sacrificed. >>

But, Nial, come not here again:
Long before dawn my soul shall be
Beyond the reach of any pain
That Modred dreams to prove on me.

Go forth thyself at dawn, and say
'This is Christ's holy natal morn,
My king is He from forth this day
When He to save mankind was born.'

Go forth and seek a lonely place
Where a great river fills the wild;
There bide, and let thy strength be grace,
And wait the Coming of a Child.

A wondrous thing shall then befall:
And when thou seek'st if it be true,
Green leaves along thy staff shall crawl,
With flowers of every lovely hue."

The monk's face whitened, like sea-foam:
Seaward he stared, and sighed "I go —
Farewell — my Lord Christ calls me home!"
Nial stooped and saw death's final throe.

An hour before the dawn he rose
And sought out Modred, brooding dumb;
"O King," he said, "my bond I close,
King Christ I seek: the Cross is come!"

Swift as a stag's leap from a height
King Modred drew his dreadful sword:
Then as a snow-wraith, silent, white,
He stared and passed without a word.

Before the flush of dawn was red
A druid came to Nial the Great:
"The doom of death hath Modred said,
Yet fears this Christ's mysterious hate:

So get you hence, you giant-thewed man:
Go your own way; come not again:
No more are you of Modred's clan:
Go now, forthwith, lest you be slain."

Nial went forth with gladsome face;
No more of Modred's clan he was:
"Now, now," he cried, "Christ's trail I'll trace,
And nowhere turn, and nowhere pause."

He laughed to think how Modred feared
The wrath of Christ, the monk's white king:
"A greater than Modred hath appeared,
To Him my sword and strength I bring."

All day, all night, he walked afar:
He saw the moon rise white and still:
The evening and the morning star:
The sunrise burn upon the hill.

He heard the moaning of the seas,
The vast sigh of the sunset plain,
The myriad surge of forest-trees;
Saw dusk and night return again.

At falling of the dusk he stood
Upon a wild and desert land:
Dark fruit he gathered for his food,
Drank water from his hollowed hand,

Cut from an ash a mighty bough
And trimmed and shaped it to the half:
"Safe in the desert am I now,
With sword," he said, "and with this staff."

The stars came out: Arcturus hung
His ice-blue fire far down the sky:
The Great Bear through the darkness swung:
The Seven Watchers rose on high.

>>

A great moon flooded all the west.
Silence came out of earth and sea
And lay upon the husht world's breast,
And breathed mysteriously.

Three hours Nial walked, three hours and more:
Then halted when beyond the plain
He stood upon that river's shore
The dying monk had bid him gain.

A little house he saw: clay-wrought,
Of wattle woven through and through:
Then, all his weariness forgot,
The joy of drowning-sleep he knew.

Three hours he slept, and then he heard
A voice — and yet a voice so low
It might have been a dreaming bird
Safe-nested by the rushing flow.

Almost he slept once more: then, *Hush!*
Once more he heard above the noise
And tempest of the river's rush
The thin faint words of a child's voice.

Good Sir, awake from sleep and dream,
Good Sir, come out and carry me,
Across this dark and raging stream
Till safe on the other side I be.

Great Nial shivered on his bed:
"No human creature calls this night,
It is a wild fetch of the dead,"
He thought, and shrunk, and shook with fright.

Once more he heard that infant-cry:
Come out, Good Sir, or else I drown —
Come out, Good Sir, or else I die
And you, too, lose a golden crown.

"A golden crown" — so Nial thought —
"No — no — not thus shall I be ta'en!
Keep, ghost-of-the-night, your crown
    gold-wrought —
Of sleep and peace I am full fain!"

Once more the windy dark was filled
With lonely cry, with sobbing plaint:
Nial's heart grew sore, its fear was stilled,
King Christ, he knew, would scorn him faint.

"Up, up thou coward, thou sluggard, thou,"
He cried, and sprang from off his bed —
"No crown thou seekest for thy brow,
But help for one in pain and dread!"

Out of the wide and lonely dark
No fetch he saw, no shape, no child:
Almost he turned again — but *hark!*
A song rose o'er the waters wild:

A King am I
Tho' a little Child,
Son of God am I,
Meek and mild,
Beautiful —
Because God hath said
Let my cup be full
Of wine and bread.

Come to me
Shaken heart,
Shaken heart!
I will not flee.
My heart
Is thy heart
O shaken heart!
Stoop to my Cup,
Sup,

>>

Drink of the wine:
The wine and the bread,
Saith God,
Are mine —
My Flesh and my Blood!

Throw thy sword in the flood:
Come, shaken heart:
Fearful thou art!
Have no more fear —
Lo, I am here,
The little One,
The Son,
Thy Lord and thy King.

It is I who sing:
Christ, your King.
Be not afraid:
Look, I am Light,
A great star
Seen from afar
In the darkness of night:
I am Light,
Be not afraid ...
Wade, wade
Into the deep flood!
Think of the Bread,
The Wine and the Bread
That are my Flesh and Blood.
Cross, cross the Flood,
Sure is the goal ...
Be not afraid
O Soul,
Be not afraid!

Nial's heart was filled with joy and pain:
"This is my king, my king indeed:
To think that drown'd in sleep I've lain
When Christ the Child-God crieth in need!"

Swift from his wattled hut he strode,
Stumbling among the grass and bent,
And, seeking where the river flowed,
Far o'er the dark flood peered and leant:

Then suddenly beside him saw
A little Child all clad in white:
He bowed his head in love and awe,
Then lifted high his burthen light.

High on his shoulders sat the Child,
While with strong limbs he fared among
The rushing waters black and wild
And where the fiercest currents swung.

The waters rose more high, more high,
Higher and higher every yard ...
Nial stumbled on with sob and sigh,
Christ heard him panting sore and hard.

"O Child," Nial cried, "forbear, forbear!
Heard you not how these waters whirled!
The weight of all the earth I bear,
The weary weight of all the world!"

Christopher! ... low above the noise,
The rush, the darkness, Nial heard
The far-off music of a Voice
That said all things in saying one word —

Christopher ... this thy name shall be!
Christ-bearer is thy Name, even so
Because of service done to me
Heavy with weight of the world's woe.

With breaking sobs, with panting breath
Christopher grasped a bent-held dune
Then with flung staff and as in death
Forward he fell in a heavy swoon. >>

All night he lay in silence there,
But safe from reach of surging tide:
White angels had him in their care,
Christ healed and watched him side by side.

When all the silver wings of dawn
Had waved above the rose-flusht east,
Christopher woke ... his dream was gone.
The angelic songs had ceased.

Was it a dream in very deed,
He wondered, broken, trembling, dazed?
His staff he lifted from the mead
And as an upright sapling raised.

Lo, it was as the monk had said —
If he would prove the vision true,
His staff would blossom to its head
With flowers of every lovely hue.

Christopher bowed: before his eyes
Christ's love fulfilled the holy hour ...
A south-wind blew, green leaves did rise
And the staff bloomed a myriad flower!

Christopher bowed in holy prayer,
While Christ's love fell like healing dew:
God's father-hand was on him there:
The peace of perfect peace he knew.

The Train to Glasgow

WILMA HORSBRUGH

Here is the train to Glasgow.

Here is the driver,
Mr MacIver,
Who drove the train to Glasgow.

Here is the guard from Donibristle
Who waved his flag and blew his whistle
To tell the driver,
Mr MacIver,
To start the train to Glasgow.

Here is a boy called Donald MacBrain
Who came to the station to catch the train
But saw the guard from Donibristle
Wave his flag and blow his whistle
To tell the driver,
Mr MacIver,
To start the train to Glasgow.

Here is the guard, a kindly man
Who, at the last moment, hauled into the van
That fortunate boy called Donald MacBrain
Who came to the station to catch the train
But saw the guard from Donibristle
Wave his flag and blow his whistle
To tell the driver,
Mr MacIver,
To start the train to Glasgow.

Here are hens and here are cocks,
Clucking and crowing inside a box,
In charge of the guard, that kindly man
Who, at the last moment, hauled into the van
That fortunate boy called Donald MacBrain
Who came to the station to catch the train

>>

But saw the guard from Donibristle
Wave his flag and blow his whistle
To tell the driver,
Mr MacIver,
To start the train to Glasgow.

Here is the train. It gave a jolt
Which loosened a catch and loosened a bolt,
And let out the hens and let out the cocks,
Clucking and crowing out of their box,
In charge of the guard, that kindly man
Who, at the last moment, hauled into the van
That fortunate boy called Donald MacBrain
Who came to the station to catch the train
But saw the guard from Donibristle
Wave his flag and blow his whistle
To tell the driver,
Mr MacIver,
To start the train to Glasgow.

The guard chased a hen and, missing it, fell.
The hens were all squawking, the cocks were as well,
And unless you were there you haven't a notion
The flurry, the fuss, the noise and commotion
Caused by the train which gave a jolt
And loosened a catch and loosened a bolt
And let out the hens and let out the cocks,
Clucking and crowing out of their box,
In charge of the guard, that kindly man
Who, at the last moment, hauled into the van
That fortunate boy called Donald MacBrain
Who came to the station to catch the train
But saw the guard from Donibristle
Wave his flag and blow his whistle
To tell the driver,
Mr MacIver,
To start the train to Glasgow.

Now Donald was quick and Donald was neat
And Donald was nimble on his feet.
He caught the hens and he caught the cocks
And he put them back in their great big box.
The guard was pleased as pleased could be
And invited Donald to come to tea
On Saturday, at Donibristle,
And let him blow his lovely whistle,
And said in all his life he'd never
Seen a boy so quick and clever,
And so did the driver,
Mr MacIver,
Who drove the train to Glasgow.

Graces

Grace

RUDOLF STEINER

As wakens the seed in the darkness of earth,
As swells the bud through the power of the air,
As ripens the fruit in the might of the sun.
So quickens the soul in the shrine of the heart
So blossoms man's spirit in the Light of the World;
So ripens man's strength in the Glory of God.

ISABEL WYATT

In root and leaf,
In flower and seed,
On Christ's body
Do I feed.
Christ be in head,
In heart, in limb,
In thought, word, deed,
Not I, but Him.

Hindi Grace

On each grain is written
The name of the eater
The giver is the one
The giver is God.

The Harvest

ALICE C. HENDERSON

The silver rain, the shining sun,
The fields where scarlet poppies run,
And all the ripples of the wheat
Are in the bread that I do eat.

So when I sit for every meal
And say a grace, I always feel
That I am eating rain and sun
And fields where scarlet poppies run.

Grace

ANONYMOUS

Before the flour the mill,
Before the mill the grain,
Before the grain, the sun, the earth, the rain,
The beauty of God's will.

Grace

CHRISTIAN MORGENSTERN

Erde die uns dies gebracht,
Sonne die es reif gemacht;
Liebe Sonne, liebe Erde
Euer nie vergessen werde.

Earth who gives to us this food;
Sun who makes it ripe and good;
Dear Sun, dear Earth, by you we live,
To you our loving thanks we give.

Three Graces

ANGELUS SILESIUS

Das Brot vom Korn
Das Korn vom Licht
Das Licht aus Gottes Angesicht.
Die Frucht der Erde
Aus Gottes Schein,
Lass Licht auch werden
Im Herzen mein.

Bread from corn
And corn from light
And light from God's own countenance.
Fruit of earth from radiance divine
May light also grow in this heart of mine.

Das Brot ernährt uns nicht
Was uns im Brote speist
Ist Gottes ew'ges Wort
Ist Leben und ist Geist.

'Tis not the bread that feeds us,
What feeds us in the bread
Is God's eternal word
Is spirit and is life.

Segne, Herr, die Gaben dieser Erde,
Dass sie deiner,
Christi Erde werde.

Bless, Lord, the gifts of this earth,
That it may become
Thine, Christ's Earth.

Prayers, Praise and Contemplation

A Child's Prayer

HENRY CHARLES BEECHING

Father, we thank Thee for the night
And for the pleasant morning light,
For rest and food and loving care,
And all that makes the world so fair.
Help us to do the thing we should,
To be to others kind and good,
In all we do, in all we say,
To grow more loving every day.

Lovely Things

H.M. SARSON

Bread is a lovely thing to eat —
God bless the barley and the wheat!

A lovely thing to breathe is air —
God bless the sunshine everywhere!

The earth's a lovely place to know —
God bless the folks that come and go!

Alive's a lovely thing to be —
Giver of life — we say — bless Thee!

Old English Prayer

FROM A SARUM PRIMER OF 1558

God be in my head,
    And in my understanding;
God be in mine eyes,
    And in my looking;
God be in my mouth,
    And in my speaking;
God be in my heart,
    And in my thinking;
God be at mine end,
    And at my departing.

Prayer of St Patrick

God be with me,
God within me,
God behind me,
God before me,
God beside me,
God around me,
God to comfort and restore me.

God beneath me,
God above me,
God in quiet,
God in danger,
God in hearts of all that love me,
God in mouth of friend and stranger.

From *The Canticle of the Sun*

ST FRANCIS OF ASSISI
Translated by Lawrence Edwards

Praised be God for brother Sun,
Who shines with splendid glow,
He brings the golden day to us
Thy glory does he show!

Praised be God for sister Moon
And every twinkling star;
They shine in heaven most bright and clear
All glorious they are.

Praised be God for brother Wind
That storms across the skies;
And then grows still, and silent moves
And sweetly sings and sighs.

Praised be God for Water pure
Her usefulness we tell.
So humble, precious, clean and good,
She works for us so well.

Praised be God for brother Fire
Friendly, and wild, and tame;
Tender and warm, mighty and strong
A flashing, flaring flame.

Praised be God for mother Earth
Who keeps us safe and well;
Whose mother heart, all warm with love,
Dark in her depths doth dwell.

The Mystic's Prayer

FIONA MACLEOD

Lay me to sleep in sheltering flame
 O Master of the Hidden Fire!
Wash pure my heart, and cleanse for me
 My soul's desire.

In flame of sunrise bathe my mind,
 O Master of the Hidden Fire,
That, when I wake, clear-eyed may be
 My soul's desire.

Evening Prayer

HERBERT HAHN

Only when I think the light
My soul begins to shine.
Only when my soul does shine
The earth becomes a star.
When the earth becomes a star
I am truly man.

Verse

CHRISTIAN MORGENSTERN

You wisdom of my higher Ego
Which spreads over me the wing
Which has led me here from the beginning
As it was the best for me.

When discouragement often fought against me
It was the discouragement of a boy;
The mature glances of the man
Have the strength to rest on you full of gratitude.

A Prayer

HERBERT HAHN

O Thou, Thou Who lighteth the World–All
Illumine me also, and take from mine eyes the blindness
That I may see Thy true Sun.
But now it is still veiled
Although it is indeed a golden sea of light
Shimmering through my soul.
And now, let me see it in the clear form of pure Truth.
And in this light let me perceive what my duties may be,
And then, when the journey is ended,
Let me reach the Holy Place.

And then, Thou, O Thou Consoler of all,
Give me also the strength actually to reach there,
And thou, O Thou Love Divine,
Receive me into Thy Kingdom and hold in purity
The Eternal Ray of True Willing.

The Lord's Prayer

Our Father which art in heaven
Hallowed be Thy name
Thy kingdom come, Thy will be done
On earth as it is in heaven.
Give us this day our daily bread
And forgive us our trespasses
As we forgive them
That trespass against us.
And lead us not into temptation
But deliver us from evil
For Thine is the Kingdom
The Power and the Glory
For ever and ever.
Amen.

The Fullness of Christ

GILES FLETCHER

He is a path, if any be misled;
He is a robe, if any naked be;
If any chance to hunger, he is bread;
If any be a bondman, he is free;
If any be but weak, how strong is he!
To dead men life he is, to sick men health;
To blind men sight, and to the needy wealth;
A pleasure without loss, a treasure without stealth.

St John the Baptist

ADAM BITTLESTON

Thou herald spirit, by the Father's grace
Abiding witness to the Light of Lights,
Look on our seeking.

All we have done on earth has left its trace,
And all we say sounds on for spirit ears.
Help at our judging.

Baptizer of the waking soul, lead out
Our lives from barren conflict in the dark
Into Christ's presence.

Let sound the music of the faithful heart,
Prophet of days to come, for brother men,
Unto Christ's glory.

Verse

HEINZ MÜLLER

'Tis Love alone can heal the Fall,
'Tis Love gives all for naught,
'Tis Love that weds Man to the All
Warms through my deed and thought.

St John the Baptist

W. DRUMMOND

The last and greatest Herald of Heaven's King
Girt with rough skins, hies to the deserts wild,
Among that savage brood the woods forth bring,
Which he more harmless found than man, and mild.

His food was locusts, and what there doth spring,
With honey that from virgin hives distill'd;
Parch'd body, hollow eyes, some uncouth thing
Made him appear, long since from earth exiled.

There burst he forth: All ye whose hopes rely
On God, with me amidst these deserts mourn,
Repent, repent, and from old errors turn!
— Who listen'd to his voice, obey'd his cry?
Only the echoes, which he made relent,
Rung from their flinty caves, Repent! Repent!

Prayer Arising out of the Needs of our Time

MICHAELOVITCH VLADIMIR LESKOFF
Translated by Marie Steiner

O Spirits, that weave in time spheres
O Spirits, that live in time streams
Spirits, that help to create the light
out of the gloom of darkness.
Hear us, we pray, that call on you
from our heart's deepest ground.
Send light-filled courage from the world of truth,
Lend humble strength to us that will to serve,
That the seeking of our soul-spirits
may be united with the Christ messenger,
He who upholds us to stand against the beast —
He who has saved us from the abyss —
That we may carry the world aims of humanity
through the darkness with courage,
That we may direct the Christ will for the earth
through the night of our time.

Celtic Prayer

O Michael Militant,
Thou King of the angels,
Shield thy people
With the power of thy sword,
Shield thy people
With the power of thy sword.

Spread thy wing
Over sea and land,
East and West,
And shield us from the foe,
East and West,
And shield us from the foe.

Brighten thy feast
From heaven above;
Be with us in the pilgrimage
And in the twistings of the fight;
Be with us in the pilgrimage
And in the twistings of the fight.

Then chief of chiefs,
Thou chief of the needy,
Be with us in the journey
And in the gleam of the river;
Be with us in the journey
And in the gleam of the river.
Thou chief of chiefs,
Thou chief of angels,
Spread thy wing
Over sea and land,
For thine is their fullness,
Thine is their fullness,
    Thine own is their fullness.
    Thine own is their fullness.

Every Atom

REX RAAB

In everything the Earth brings forth
the Christ's own spirit is;
There is no atom in the World
that He has not made His.

Oh, artist, priest and engineer!
bless each thing with your touch!
Give all your heart and soul to Him!
Is that so very much?

Blue and Rose

ISABEL WYATT

Little son,
Whence comes blue?
It comes when dark is shone into.
Because the Sun's fair golden Light
Shines down into my body's night,
My cloak is blue,
My little son.

Little son,
Whence comes rose?
It comes when light through darkness glows.
Because the Sun's fair golden spark
Is shining from my body dark,
My robe is rose,
My little son.

Song

TRADITIONAL

Over the earth is a mantle of green
Over the green the dew
Over the dew are the arching trees
Over the trees the blue.
Across the blue the scudding clouds
Over the clouds the sun,
Over it all is the love of God
Blessing us every one.

Praise

MOLLY DE HAVAS

Very early every morning
All the birds awake and sing,
Praising God that now the sunrise
Warmth and light to earth will bring.

When the evening dusk is falling
Loud and sweet again they sing,
Praising God that now the sunset
Dark and quiet sleep will bring.

We His children also thank Him,
Lift our hearts and gladly sing;
For His gifts of light and darkness
Work and sleep, our praise we bring.

Verse

OWEN BARFIELD

Fruit in a blossom,
And petals in a seed,
Reeds in a river bed,
And music in a reed:
Stars in a firmament
Shining in the night,
Sun in a galaxy,
And planet in its light;
Bones in the rosy blood
Like land in the sea.
Marrow in a skeleton,
And I in me.

I Love all Beauteous Things

ROBERT BRIDGES

I love all beauteous things,
    I seek and adore them;
God hath no better praise,
And man in his hasty days
    Is honoured for them.

I too will something make
    And joy in the making;
Altho' tomorrow it seem
Like the empty words of a dream
    Remembered on waking.

Alleluia for All Things

ALFRED CECIL HARWOOD

Of all created things, of earth and sky,
Of God and Man, things lowly and things high,
We sing this day with thankful hearts and say,
Alleluia! Alleluia!

Of Light and Darkness and the colours seven
Stretching their rainbow bridge from earth to heaven,
We sing this day ...

Of Sun and Moon, the lamps of Night and Day,
Stars and Planets sounding on their way,
We sing this day ...

Of Times and Seasons, evening, and fresh morn,
Of Birth and Death, green blade and corn,
We sing this day ...

Of all that lives and moves, the Winds a-blow,
Fire and old Ocean's never resting flow,
We sing this day ...

Of Earth and from Earth's darkness springing free,
The flowers outspread, the Heavenward-reaching tree,
We sing this day ...

Of creatures all, the Eagle in his flight,
The patient Ox, the Lion that trusts his might,
We sing this day ...

Of Man with hand outstretched for service high,
Courage at heart, truth in his steadfast eye,
We sing this day ...

Of Angels and Archangels, Spirits clear,
Warders of Souls and Watchers of the year.
We sing this day ...

Of God made Man and through Man sacrificed,
Of Man through love made God, Adam made Christ.
We sing this day ...

Children's Birthday Song

ALFRED CECIL HARWOOD

Many the stars that stand over the earth,
    And the days as the years go by,
But one star over the place of my birth,
    One hour, when first was I,
Looked for the light where the new child lay,
    Listened and heard the sign,
And the great sun rose on my life's first day,
    And the glory of earth was mine.

Fine things, O Earth, you have shown to me,
    Rare things from you I have heard,
The laughter of light on the splendid sea,
    The song of the covert bird;
And I have dreamed with the dreaming rose
    Whose slumber the butterfly shakes,
And wakened and watched with the silent snows
    When the whole world watches and wakes.

And once and again in the dance of the days
    Leaps out my day and my hour,
And I see above me the one star blaze,
    And its presence I feel like a Power.
And I say to that steadfast star I see,
    "O star, be my light like thine,
The sun in the heavens thy comfort be,
    And the Christ on earth be mine."

TRADITIONAL

Monday's child is fair of face
Tuesday's child is full of grace,
Wednesday's child is full of woe,
Thursday's child has far to go,
Friday's child is loving and giving,
Saturday's child works hard for a living
And the child that is born on the Sabbath day
Is bonny and blithe, and good and gay.

Selfhood Discovered

MARGARET GUDEMIAN

Knee-deep in a field of buttercups
Surrounded by light and gold
Far off in my childhood playtime
I witnessed my Ego unfold.

Lost to the laughter of playmates
Startled, I knew myself grown
Separate in my existence —
Different, uniquely alone.

Alone with the buttercups shining
In golden splendour around;
Alone, in that holy moment
With the sunlight streaming down.

Wisdom and truth eternal
Flashed through my tremulous heart
As I stood there in time suspended
Consciously stood apart.

Children's voices calling
Brought me to earth again,
I carried my secret knowledge
Wrapped in my seven year frame.

Long since that magical moment
But radiant the memory will stay —
How the sun and the light and the buttercups
Shone round me that hallowed day.

Seeking

MARGARET GUDEMIAN

Sometimes, I almost touch
With my hand
That which Man strives
To understand —
In the radiant freshness
Of a singing dawn
Or when I stand
In awe
Before
The flaming glory of the sunset.
When with leaping heart I behold
The shining promise
Of the Bow
I almost know;
I strain my ears
To hear the language of the spheres.
With tremulous heart
I wait
Anticipate
The flooding of my soul
With the deep secrets of
The Universe.
I nurse
And cherish a hope.
These moments pass
And I must look through glass
darkly a little longer
Albeit growing stronger
In the belief that one day
I shall know
My heart will flow
In harmony with all creation;
A veil will lift
And the divine gift
Of understanding
Will flood my soul
And make me whole!

To the Butterfly

MARGARET GUDEMIAN

Creature of light! How my heart sings
As past you flutter on shimmering wings,
Unfettered by the chains of Earth.
Metamorphosed to joyous birth!
Living in regions of the Sun,
Reflecting memories of life begun —
Emerging from the chrysalis
Free in the radiant cosmic bliss!
Seeking for your nourishment
Only the finest supplement
Offered with pleasure by that other
Blessing of Nature, the flower, your brother;
Communing with the Angeloi
A miracle of fluttering joy!
You speak to me of things which are to be —
You bear the stamp of Immortality!

From *The Book of Life*

The Eternal reigneth, the Eternal hath reigned,
the Eternal shall reign for ever and ever.
Blessed be the name of His glorious kingdom for ever and ever.
The Eternal is the only God. He is my rock, in whom there is no iniquity.
The Eternal hath given, and the Eternal hath taken away.
Blessed art Thou, O Eternal, the Reviver of the dead.

From *A Prose Hymn*

ALFRED THE GREAT

Hate evil and flee from it!
Love virtue and follow it!
Whatsoever you do is always done before the
Eternal and Almighty God.
He seeth all, and all he judges and will requite.

Worldly Wise

TRADITIONAL

For want of a nail
The shoe was lost,
For want of a shoe
The horse was lost,
For want of a horse
The rider was lost.

For want of a rider
The battle was lost,
For want of a battle
The kingdom was lost,
And all for the want
Of a horse shoe nail.

From *Auguries of Innocence*

WILLIAM BLAKE

Man was made for Joy and Woe;
And when this we rightly know,
Thro the world we safely go
... Joy and Woe are woven fine
A Clothing for the Soul divine
Under every grief and pine
Runs a joy with silken twine ...

From *The Tree of Life — The Mystery*

RALPH HODGSON

He came and took me by the hand
Up to a red rose tree,
He kept his meaning to himself
But gave the rose to me.

I did not pray him to lay bare
The mystery to me,
Enough the rose was heaven to smell
And His own face to see.

The Fairy Story of Good and Evil

From *The Soul's Probation*

RUDOLF STEINER

Once upon a time there lived a man
who pondered much about the world.
His mind was tortured most of all
By his desire to know the origin of evil;
He could not give himself an answer.
"The world has come from God," he said to himself
"And God can only have the good within him,
Then how do evil men come from the good?"
Ever and ever again he pondered all in vain,
He could not find the answer.

One day, it happened that this brooding thinker
Upon his way beheld a tree
Which was in conversation with an axe.
"And mark!" The axe was saying to the tree:
"What is impossible for you I can do it;
I can fell you, but you, not me."
Thereon the tree said to the haughty axe:
"A year ago a man cut from my body
With another axe, the very wood
From which he fashioned then your handle."

And when the man had heard this speech
A thought arose within his soul
Which, though he could not put it into words,
Gave satisfying answer to the question
How evil can arise from out of good.

Composed Upon Westminster Bridge

WILLIAM WORDSWORTH

Earth has not anything to show more fair:
Dull would he be of soul who could pass by
A sight so touching in its majesty:
This City now doth, like a garment, wear
The beauty of the morning; silent, bare,
Ships, towers, domes, theatres and temples lie
Open unto the fields, and to the sky;
All bright and glittering in the smokeless air.
Never did sun more beautifully steep
In his first splendour, valley, rock, or hill;
Ne'er saw I, never felt, a calm so deep!
The river glideth at his own sweet will:
Dear God! the very houses seem asleep;
And all that mighty heart is lying still!

My Heart Leaps up

WILLIAM WORDSWORTH

My heart leaps up when I behold
    A rainbow in the sky:
So was it when my life began;
So is it now I am a man;
So be it when I shall grow old,
    Or let me die!
The Child is father of the Man;
And I could wish my days to be
Bound each to each by natural piety.

EDWARD MATCHETT

Let us make a thing of beauty
That long may live when we are gone;
Let us make a thing of beauty
That hungry souls may feast upon;

Whether it be wood or marble,
Music, art or poetry,
Let us make a thing of beauty
To help set Man's bound spirit free.

With My Words

DAVID KUHRT

In ordered correspondence with the earth
the hierarchies of Heaven sleep,
enchanted in the stones
the flowers and sentient things.
Glistening in the vein of ore,
resplendent in a rose,
I see a universe sustained by deity enthralled;
and with my words I liberate
all this pains-taking enchantment.

Stones, Rivers, Cliffs or Trees

DAVID KUHRT

If there are angels
think of them,
do not enunciate the word.
Stones, rivers, cliffs or trees
respond if I call
but no angel appears.
They are the winged thoughts
bringing the things to me.
I gather them beyond.

Stones, rivers, cliffs or trees,
together we are tangible.
Falling, like Adam, into divergence
the angels hold us centered,
our thoughts like stars.

Stones, rivers, cliffs or trees
he named them, forgetting God
whose fragments they are.
If you will remember Him
do not enunciate the word.
In stones, rivers, cliffs or trees
He is bystander
to his own recovery.

Love's Philosophy

PERCY BYSSHE SHELLEY

The fountains mingle with the river
　　And the rivers with the Ocean,
The winds of Heaven mix for ever
　　With a sweet emotion;
Nothing in the world is single;
　　All things by a law divine
In one spirit meet and mingle.
　　Why not I with thine? —

See the mountains kiss high Heaven
　　And the waves clasp one another;
No sister-flower would be forgiven
　　If it disdained its brother;
And the sunlight clasps the earth
　　And the moonbeams kiss the sea:
What is all this sweet work worth
　　If thou kiss not me?

A Nation's Greatness

RALPH WALDO EMERSON

Not gold, but only men can make
A people great and strong —
Men who, for truth and honour's sake,
Stand fast and suffer long.
Brave men who work while others sleep,
Who dare while others fly —
They build a nation's pillars deep,
And raise them to the sky.

From *A Dialogue between the Resolute Soul and Created Pleasure*

ANDREW MARVELL

Courage, my Soul, now learn to wield
The weight of thine immortal shield.
Close on thy head thy helmet bright.
Balance thy sword against the fight.
See where an army, strong as fair,
With silken banners spreads the air.
Now, if thou be'st that thing divine,
In this day's combat let it shine:
And show that Nature wants an art
To conquer one resolvèd heart.

A Poem

MALTBIE DAVENPORT BABCOCK

Be strong!
We are not here to play, to dream, to drift;
We have hard work to do, and loads to lift;
Shun not the struggle — face it; 'tis God's gift.

Be strong!
Say not, "The days are evil. Who's to blame?"
And fold the hands and acquiesce — oh shame!
Stand up, speak out, and bravely, in God's name.

Be strong!
It matters not how deep entrenched the wrong;
How hard the battle goes, the day how long;
Faint not — fight not! Tomorrow comes the song.

Friends

TRADITIONAL

We do not make our friends, we find them only
Where they have waited for us many years;
One day we wander forth when feeling lonely
And lo! a comrade at our side appears.
'tis not discovery, 'tis recognition —
A smile, a glance, and then we grasp the hand —
No explanation needed, no condition
That we are friends is all we understand.

Onward and Upward

JOHN CHARLES EARLE

I pass the vale. I breast the steep.
I bear the cross: the cross bears me.
Light leads me on to light. I weep
For joy at what I hope to see
When, scaled at last the arduous height,
For every painful step I trod,
I traverse worlds on worlds of light,
And pierce some deeper depths of God.

From *The Second Book of Macrocosmos and Microcosmos*

BERNARDUS SYLVESTRIS OF CHARTRES

Now last and joyfullest creation of my hands,
Let man arise!
Akin to the Gods, and an image of the Gods.
Let him receive his spirit from the heavens,
His body from the elements.
Let him dwell upon the earth with his body.
Let him dwell with his spirit in the Heights.
These are the two poles of his being.
Thus at one and the same time he shall serve both divine and earthly;
He shall share with the Holy Ones of Heaven the gift of reason,
Naught but a little line shall separate man from God.
The mindless beasts have senses that are dull and dim,
Forward their jowls are pointed, and downward they bend their glance.
The countenance of man alone bears witness to the Majesty of the Spirit,
He alone lifts his head in holiness to the stars,
Gazing upon Heaven's laws, and the inviolable movements of its heights,
That he may know them as the pattern of his life.
He shall see whence cometh the bright shining of Phoebus and the Muses.
Whence the quaking of the earth and the tumult of the seas;
He shall know why the summer days are long,
And the summer nights go shrunken to small hours.
That the elements be his, I will;
That fire shall glow for him, Sun illumine him,
Earth seeds germinate for him,
Waters flow for him.
I will;
That the earth shall bear fruit for him,
The waters bear fish for him,
The mountains bear cattle for him,
The forest shall bring him the wild beasts.
He shall subdue all things.

He shall rule the earth; he shall create dominions.
Thus I appoint him overlord of all things, and their priest.
But when he shall sink down and shall have fulfilled his days,
When his bodily dwelling place shall crumble away,
Then shall man rise up to the ether;
He shall rise, not as an unknown friendless stranger,
But he shall attain to the sign and the place of his Star.

Word Made Flesh

KATHLEEN RAINE

Word whose breath is the world-circling atmosphere,
Word that utters the world, that turns the wind,
Word that articulates the bird that speeds upon the air.

Word that blazes out the trumpet of the sun,
Whose silence is the violin-music of the stars,
Whose melody is the dawn, and harmony the night.

Word traced in water of lakes, and light on water
Light on still water, moving water, waterfall
And water colours of cloud, of dew, of spectral rain.

Word inscribed on stone, mountain range upon range of stone,
Word that is fire of the sun and fire within
Order of atmos, crystalline symmetry.

Grammar of five-fold rose and six fold lily,
Spiral of leaves on a bough, helix of shells,
Rotation of twining plants on axes of darkness and light.

Instinctive wisdom of fish and lion and ram,
Rhythm of generation in flagellate and fern,
Flash of fin, beat of wing, heartbeat, beat of the dance.

Hieroglyph in whose exact precision is defined
Feather and insect wing, refraction of multiple eyes.
Eyes of the creatures, oh myriadfold vision of the world.

Statement of mystery, how shall we name
A spirit clothed in world, a world made man?

At a Solemn Music

JOHN MILTON

Blest pair of Sirens, pledges of heav'n's joy,
Sphere-born harmonious sisters, Voice and Verse,
Wed your divine sounds, and mixed power employ
Dead things with inbreathed sense able to pierce,
And to our high-raised phantasy present
That undisturbèd song of pure content,
Aye sung before the sapphire-coloured throne
To him that sits thereon,
With saintly shout and solemn jubilee,
Where the bright Seraphim in burning row
Their loud uplifted angel-trumpets blow,
And the Cherubic host in thousand quires
Touch their immortal harps of golden wires,
With those just spirits that wear victorious palms,
Hymns devout and holy psalms
Singing everlastingly;
That we on earth with undiscording voice
May rightly answer that melodious noise;
As once we did, till disproportioned sin
Jarred against Nature's chime, and with harsh din
Broke the fair music that all creatures made
To their great Lord, whose love their motion swayed
In perfect diapason, whilst they stood
In first obedience and their state of good.
O may we soon again renew that song,
And keep in tune with heav'n, till God ere long
To his celestial consort us unite,
To live with him, and sing in endless morn of light.

Lied from Heinrich von Ofterdingen

NOVALIS
Translated by David Kuhrt

Wake up in singularity
You children of all time.
Leave now your resting places.
For soon it will be light.

I take your threads and spin them
To make a single strand.
Our flesh is all dependent,
One life in every land.

Each lives in all the others
The whole in every part.
One breath of life shall move us
To singleness of heart.

Nothing if not soul is yours
All dream and mystery.
Go strongly into darkness,
And tease the Holy Three.

ALBERT STEFFEN

O let us build a ship for Christ's disciples,
Set sail to seek His visage through the dark —
For mankind in the cradle and the coffin
And for the blissful in the sun's bright barque.

The cross, her anchor, rudder — the Spirit's ray!
O brother, sister — you, to steer the way!
And guiltless or guilty, we who sail from land
Shall know the mercy of His saving hand.

From *A Song for St Cecilia's Day, 1687*

JOHN DRYDEN

From Harmony, from heav'nly Harmony
This universal Frame began.
When Nature underneath a heap
    Of jarring Atomes lay,
And cou'd not heave her Head,
The tuneful Voice was heard from high,
    Arise ye more than dead.
Then cold, and hot, and moist, and dry,
In order to their stations leap,
    And Musick's pow'r obey.

From Harmony, from heav'nly Harmony
This universal frame began:
From Harmony to Harmony
Through all the compass of the Notes it ran,
The Diapason closing full in Man.

From *An Essay on Man*

ALEXANDER POPE

All are but parts of one stupendous whole,
Whose body Nature is, and God the soul;
That, changed through all, and yet in all the same,
Great in the earth, as in th' ethereal frame,
Warms in the sun, refreshes in the breeze,
Glows in the stars, and blossoms in the trees,
Lives through all life, extends through all extent,
Spreads undivided, operates unspent ...

All nature is but art, unknown to thee;
All chance, direction, which thou canst not see;
All discord, harmony, not understood;
All partial evil, universal good:
And, spite of pride, in erring reason's spite,
One truth is clear, WHATEVER IS, IS RIGHT!

Loss

The loss of gold is much
The loss of time is more
The loss of Christ is such
As no man can restore.

Marvel

All things are marvellous
If only we look well.
Is the little seed more marvellous,
Or roses! Who can tell?

From *Paradise Lost* Book Twelve

JOHN MILTON

The brandish'd sword of God before them blazed
Fierce as a comet; which with torrid heat,
And vapour as the Libyan air adust,
Began to parch that temperate clime; whereat
In either hand the hast'ning Angel caught
Our ling'ring parents, and to th' eastern gate
Led them direct, and down the cliff as fast
To the subjected plain; then disappeared.
They looking back, all th' eastern side beheld
Of Paradise, so late their happy seat,
Waved over by that flaming brand, the gate
With dreadful faces thronged and fiery arms.
Some natural tears they dropped, but wiped them soon;
The world was all before them, where to choose
Their place of rest, and Providence their guide:
They hand in hand with wand'ring steps and slow,
Through Eden took their solitary way.

A Creed

JOHN MASEFIELD

I hold that when a person dies
    His soul returns again to earth
Arrayed in some new flesh-disguise;
    Another mother gives him birth;
With sturdier limbs and brighter brain
The old soul takes the road again.

Such is my own belief and trust,
    This hand, this hand that takes the pen,
Has many a hundred times been dust
    And turned as dust to dust again.
These eyes of mine have blinked and shone
In Thebes, in Troy and Babylon.

All that I rightly think or do,
    Or make or spoil, or bless or blast,
Is curse or blessing justly due
    For sloth or effort in the past.
My life's a statement of the sum
Of vice indulged, or overcome.

I know that in my lives to be
    My sorry heart will ache and burn
And worship unavailingly
    The woman whom I used to spurn,
And shake to see another have
The love I spurned, the love she gave.

And I shall know, in angry words,
    In gibes and mocks, and many a tear,
A carrion flock of homing birds,
    The gibes and scorns I uttered here.
The brave word that I failed to speak
Will brand me dastard on the cheek.

And as I wander on the roads
    I shall be helped and healed and blessed;
Kind words shall cheer and be as goads
    To urge to heights before unguessed.
My road shall be the road I made;
All that I gave shall be repaid.

So shall I fight, so shall I tread,
    In this long war beneath the stars;
So shall a glory wreathe my head,
    So shall I faint and show the scars,
Until this case, the clogging mould
Be smithied all to kingly gold.

Love

GEORGE HERBERT

Love bade me welcome: yet my soul drew back,
    Guilty of dust and sin.
But quick-eyed Love, observing me grow slack
    From my first entrance in,
Drew nearer to me, sweetly questioning,
    If I lacked anything.

"A guest," I answered, "worthy to be here."
    Love said, "You shall be he."
"I, the unkind, ungrateful? Ah my dear,
    I cannot look on thee."
Love took my hand, and smiling did reply,
    "Who made the eyes but I?"

"Truth Lord, but I have marred them: let my shame
    Go where it doth deserve."
"And know you not," says Love, "who bore the blame?"
    "My dear, then I will serve."
"You must sit down," says Love, "and taste my meat."
    So I did sit and eat.

MARGARET MORGAN

I can't believe I never knew
The truth of what I thought was true;
I can't believe I never thought
To question what I had been taught;
God grant I keep an open mind,
To seek —
And learn from what I find.

Verses and Meditations for Teachers

The Awakening Call of Michael

RUDOLF STEINER
Translated by John Davy

Wir Menschen der Gegenwart
Brauchen das rechte Gehör
Fur des Geistes Morgenruf,
Den Morgenruf des Michael.
Geist-Erkenntnis will
Der Seele erschliessen
Dies wahre Morgenruf-Hören.

We people of today
Need a true ear
For the Spirit's awakening call —
The awakening call of Michael.
Spiritual-knowing seeks
To open the soul
To a true hearing
Of this awakening call.

CHRISTIAN MORGENSTERN

I have fathomed the nature of Man
    and studied his maker's art
I now perceive the World
    down to its very heart
Its inmost purpose is Love, I know,
And I am here in Love to grow and grow.

RUDOLF STEINER

My head bears the being
    of the resting Stars.
My Breast harbours the life
    of the wandering Stars.
My Body lives and moves
    amid the Elements.
        This am I.

A Teacher's Thoughts for his Children

RUDOLF STEINER

You who out of heaven's brightness
Now descend to earthly darkness
Thus through life's resisting forces;
Spirit radiance to unfold
Spirit warmness to enkindle
Spirit forces to call forth —
Be you warmed through by my love
Radiant thinking
Tranquil feeling
Healing willing —
That in spirit's heights well rooted
And in earth's foundations working
You may servants of the Word become
Spirit illumining
Love evoking
Being strengthening.

To Wonder at Beauty

RUDOLF STEINER

To wonder at beauty,
Stand guard over truth,
Revere what is noble,
Resolve on the good.
This leadeth man truly
To purpose in living,
To justice in dealing,
To peace in his feeling,
To light in his thinking;
And teaches him trust
In the ruling of God,
In all that exists
In the widths of the world,
In the depths of the soul.

From *The Essentials of Education*

RUDOLF STEINER

Dem Stoff sich verschreiben,
Heißt Seelen zerreiben,
Im Geiste sich finden,
Heißt Menschen verbinden.
Im Menschen sich schauen,
Heißt Welten erbauen.

To bind the Self to matter
Means to shatter souls.
To find oneself in the Spirit
Means to unite mankind.
To behold the Self in man
Means to build worlds.

For Inner Tranquillity

RUDOLF STEINER
Translated by George and Mary Adams

Quiet I bear within me.
I bear within myself
Forces to make me strong.
Now will I be imbued
With their glowing warmth.
Now will I fill myself
With my own will's resolve.
And I will feel the quiet
Pouring through all my being,
When by my steadfast striving
I become strong
To find within myself
The source of strength,
The strength of inner quiet.

For Courage

RUDOLF STEINER
Translated by George and Mary Adams

We must eradicate from the soul all fear and terror
Of what comes to meet us from the future.
We must look forward with absolute equanimity to
Whatever comes and we must think only that
Whatever comes is given us by a world direction full of wisdom.
It is part of what we must learn in this age,
Namely to act out of pure trust in the ever-present
help of spiritual worlds.
Truly, nothing else will do if our courage is not to fail us.
Let us discipline our will and let us seek the
Awakening from within ourselves, every morning and every evening.

For Selflessness

RUDOLF STEINER
Translated by George and Mary Adams

Spirit triumphant
Send flame through the weakness of timorous souls.
Burn up the "I" lust,
Kindle compassion
That selflessness, the life-stream of Mankind
May rule as the well-spring
Of spiritual rebirth.

For the Dead

RUDOLF STEINER
Translated by George and Mary Adams

May love of hearts reach out to love of souls,
May warmth of love ray out to Spirit-light.
Even so would we draw near to you,
Thinking with you Thoughts of Spirit,
Feeling in you the Love of Worlds,
Consciously at one with you
Willing in silent Being.

Ecce Homo

RUDOLF STEINER

In the heart the loom of feeling,
In the head the light of thinking,
In the limbs the strength of will.
Weaving of radiant light,
Strength of the weaving,
Light of the surging strength,
Lo, this is Man.

I'm on a Committee!

ANONYMOUS

Oh, give me your pity, I'm on a committee,
Which means that from morning to night
We attend, and amend, and contend, and defend,
Without a conclusion in sight.

We confer and concur, we defer and demur,
And reiterate all of our thoughts.
We revise the agenda with frequent addenda,
And consider a load of reports.

We compose and propose, we support and oppose,
And the points of procedure are fun!
But though various notions are brought up as motions,
There's terribly little gets done.

We resolve and absolve, but we never dissolve,
Since it's out of the question for us.
What a shattering pity to end our committee,
Where else could we make such a fuss.

Index